OPERATION HIPPO

Massacre and nightmare carnage in Idi Amin's Uganda . . . high-tension scenes of pursuit, murder and sexual brutality in London . . . a vicious white mercenary in a bizarre alliance with black African exiles . . . the most senior members of the British Government caught in one of the most difficult diplomatic dilemmas of the decade – these are just some of the elements in the most compelling and explosive assassination thriller of the year: James Konrad's TARGET AMIN.

*Here is a story of political violence, intrigue and treachery so topical that it makes Frederick Forsyth look like ancient history!*

# *Target Amin*

**JAMES KONRAD**

SPHERE BOOKS LIMITED
30/32 Gray's Inn Road, London WC1X 8JL

First published in Sphere Books Ltd 1977


*To*
*L. S-E.*

TRADE MARK

Set in Linotype Times

Printed in Great Britain by
C. Nicholls & Company Ltd
The Philips Park Press, Manchester

'God will always bless me. I will not die until the day when God wants me to die'.
*His Excellency Al-Haji Field Marshal Dr. Idi Amin Dada, V.C., D.S.O., M.C., President for Life.*

'God will return to Uganda one day'.
*A Ugandan exile.*

*Part One*

# MASSACRE AT MAKERERE

## ONE

*Tuesday, 3rd August, 1976*

It was well after 9.00 by the time Michael Kinkasa climbed the steps to the Administration Building and with a curt nod to the janitor turned left down Dettol-fresh corridors towards the lecture hall. He was late. It irritated him because the lecture he had prepared on D. H. Lawrence would have needed a full hour to deliver. The reason for his being late was that *kondos* had stolen his bicycle during the night. He had chained it to Mrs. Mukasa's dustbin but they had stolen that too and he had never heard a thing. As a result he had been forced to walk to the campus, setting out before breakfast with the sluggish streams of workers who every morning filled the approach roads to the city, shuffling into work, cowed, sweaty and silent, while overhead the kites and Marabou storks circled in search of the easiest pickings offered by the new day.

He had not enjoyed walking with them, the Mr. Nobodies wearing white shirts and carrying battered briefcases, the turbaned women with bundles of cassia twigs on their heads and the tight-bottomed girls with their flip-flops and greased legs. They were the ordinary people and on this bicycleless morning they annoyed him. Students and staff at Makerere were encouraged now to live off the campus so as to be in touch with the reality of these wretched lives, part of the official line that the University should commit itself to nation-building, to readjusting its curricula to Uganda's needs. In principle Michael Kinkasa agreed with Africanisation, but few of the students had the money to live out and, although Michael still denied it, living in downtown Kampala meant living in fear.

In the five years he had been away the city had changed. The green residential areas on Kampala's hilltops, where attractive bungalows stood behind their trim hedges and lawned gardens – in colonial days the exclusive preserve of Europeans and wealthy Indians – had already been taken over by the African élite, the *Wabenzi* (as the owners of Mercedes-Benz cars were jealously known) before he left. But now it was not the civil servants, mostly Baganda like himself, who enjoyed these privileges and, as he had been brought up to believe, deservedly so, but the military men, uneducated louts from the northern tribes who drove their cars and trucks through the hedges and over the flowerbeds and whose ignorant women were turning their once-elegant villas into derelict shanties. Perhaps Michael saw these things through the eyes of one dispossessed, though it was some time ago now that his own family had lived in splendour in one of the large and beautiful homes on Nakasero Hill.

His father had been a minister in the short-lived Democratic Party Government of 1961 during the days of political experiment when the Baganda had tried briefly for independence before Obote swept to power. At the time, an impressionable and arrogant youth of fifteen, Michael had been sorry to leave the grandeur and comfort of their Kampala existence and to return with his family to their homestead in the small village of Ntemkoge, a ragged bunch of huts in the coffee-growing country of Masaka. He had felt ashamed to see his father retire so readily to his ancestral and almost meaningless rôle of chief of a small tribe and to living happily again among his grandchildren, his cows, his chickens and his goats. But Michael felt some relief now that his father was out of Kampala and had faded altogether from the political scene. After the coup that toppled Obote there had been a chance for him to make a come-back, but he was already an old man by then and wisely had chosen to stay away.

His father's eclipse had not hindered Michael's own career. After completing his education at a boarding school in Kampala and a year at Makerere College he had won a scholarship to London University. Life in Britain had suited Michael's gentle, easy-going nature and once he became accustomed to the climate he had settled into a happy if typical student's existence – though at the age of thirty he was more serious about his studies than most. In his last year he had worked hard to get a good degree in English. The offer to come back and teach at Makerere had arrived at a time when for personal reasons he wanted a change, to get away from London for a while. Otherwise he would not have decided to return, for although he refused to believe everything he heard or read in the papers about Amin's Uganda, he knew that in the years that he had been away the country which Winston Churchill had once described as 'the pearl of Africa' had lost something of its lustre. But at least, he told himself, Uganda now belonged to Africans, and in the month that he had been back Michael, who was more attuned to the poetry of Blake than to the reality of tribal politics, had tried to keep to the mild optimism of that opinion, even if it meant closing his eyes and ears to what was going on all around him.

To begin with, Michael ignored the chaos caused by shortages, the frightening uncertainty of rocketing prices, the hunger that stalked the hovels of the poorer African suburbs where children and mangy dogs alike rooted through piles of garbage for something to eat. He tried to pretend that fear was an illusion, that the stories told by his students of persecutions at Makerere were wild exaggerations. He even persuaded himself that the tanks that rolled along Kampala Road chewing up the tarmac like liquorice were serving a useful purpose, that the men from the Public Safety Unit in their dark glasses, platform shoes and bell-bottomed trousers who stepped out of the shadows to ask you your business were genuinely concerned with public safety, with protecting the public from the scores of young hooligans who hung about the street corners during the day and after dark prowled the city in sinister and desperate gangs. Disappearances, cries in the night, the staccato bursts of machine-gun fire, even the grisly evidence of bloated bodies washed up on to the beaches of Lake Victoria – which he had seen with his own eyes – were not enough to convince him of the truth. Michael preferred not to think about such things. He concentrated rather on his work, determined to avoid at all costs 'getting involved.' But after a month of living in the city the strain was beginning to tell, cracks were appearing in the thin shell that encased his conscience. The theft of his bicycle, an old bone-shaking Raleigh for which he had paid half his first month's salary, although in itself a trivial incident, had stirred in him a deep unspecific resentment. He felt angry with the whole world that morning, but most of all with himself, for now he guiltily regretted his decision to return to the land of his forefathers.

The notice pinned to the door of the lecture hall did nothing to improve Michael's humour. He did not read beyond the word 'BOYCOTT,' but turned and swiftly retraced his steps along the corridor which now for the first time he noticed was completely deserted. At the main door he asked the janitor in peremptory tones for an explanation of the students' absence, as if the man himself was somehow responsible for their not being there. The janitor, a stolid-looking Basoga with unblinking eyes, sat his ground and did not answer. Slowly lifting his large hands from the desk he turned up pale leathery palms and then replaced them. Furious, Michael repeated his question. His students claimed that the janitor was one of the 'intelligence' officers recently posted on the campus, mostly in the guise of maintenance men or librarians, to spy on their activities – a suggestion that he had promptly dismissed as ridiculous. Now in his anger he was not so sure. This time the man replied: 'You will find them down on Freedom Square, but if you go with them you will only bring trouble on your head.'

Ignoring the janitor's advice, Michael ran from the building, scarcely knowing why he ran but suddenly overwhelmed by an impending sense of disaster. He emerged from under the arched doorway and stopped for a second between its lantern-topped pillars: standing quite still in the bright sunshine, blinking out over the green and peaceful campus fringed with golden cassias, he remembered what he had seen earlier. At the time he had made little of it, but on his way up Makerere Hill earlier that morning he had noticed an armoured troop carrier parked in a lane between the banana tree *shambas* and the broken-down sheds of the slums that encroached upon the University compound. The vehicle was full of soldiers with automatic weapons slung about their shoulders and their camouflaged legs dangling over the sides, laughing and joking with a fat Bible-black whore, who signalled coyly to them from the doorway of her verminous shack. Michael had walked by, turning his head as much from the stench of rotting rubbish and stale urine as to avoid the incurious gaze of the soldiers. Now as he set off again at a fast trot along the concrete walkway that led between the student halls of residence, he understood with growing dismay the meaning of their jovial, almost disinterested presence. And with this realisation, which called to the surface all the suppressed doubts and fears of his deliberate refusal to recognise the evil that had overtaken the country during his years in voluntary exile, he thought little of his own safety, only of the need to warn.

## TWO

In the basin of Freedom Square, a grass and concrete declivity surrounded on four sides by modern university buildings, more than two thousand Makerere students had gathered to hold a meeting to protest against the enrolment of police spies by the University and to discuss the continued boycott of lectures. In order to lend dignity to the proceedings most of them wore their scarlet university gowns, which against white shirts and black skins gave them a festive, almost carnival appearance that was none the less impressive. The crowd stood still and silent to listen to a young, light-skinned man with a short 'Makerere' beard, who stood on a grassy bank raised above their heads and addressed the students calmly in short precise sentences. His voice, unamplified, carried easily to the furthest corners of the enclosed square: there was no-one present who was not closely interested in what he had to say.

The speaker recounted, as if he were listing the achievements of the academic year, the series of events which had brought them together on that August morning to stand again in defiance of President Amin, whom he described as 'a mass murderer and destroyer of Uganda's economy.' Opposition to Amin and his killer squads had been consistent at Makerere ever since he came to power in the military coup of 1971. But the crisis which they now faced had begun in earnest on the 23rd January, 1976.

A Uganda army captain, after insulting the students on the Makerere campus, had shot and killed a girl student at the nearby Kololo Secondary School and seriously wounded three others who had answered him back with a slap after being similarly insulted. The Makerere students had at once written a letter of protest to Amin, as Chancellor of the University, asking that the captain should be demoted. The day after receiving their letter, Amin had promoted the man to the rank of major for being 'a very brave soldier.'

The next development in the confrontation had occurred at the University's graduation ball on the 5th March, 1976. Paul Serwanga, a third-year law student had gone to the dance with his fiancée, a pretty trainee nurse at Mulago Hospital. The captain, or major as he had now become, was interested in the girl and had sent three of his men to the dance to fetch her back for him, but the students had ganged together and refused to let them into the ballroom. The major's men, however, lay in wait for the couple and shot Paul Serwanga dead as he was taking the girl home.

The following day the students held a meeting on the campus and called for the overthrow of Amin. Anywhere they could find them they tore down pictures of the 'Gen' and burned them, burying the ashes in a shallow grave. Then in their bright red gowns they marched through the streets of Kampala shouting anti-Amin slogans. Their numbers were swelled by people in the street who joined them, cautiously to begin with, for this was the first mass public demonstration against Amin, but as the size of the crowd grew, more boldly. By the time they reached the central post office they were several thousand strong.

Now Amin was forced to act. 'From a genuine desire to learn the truth,' as some said, he appointed a commission of enquiry under the chairmanship of Professor Brian Langlands, a British academic at Makerere, to investigate the death of Paul Serwanga. The work of the commission was allowed to proceed normally until it began a secondary enquiry into the disappearance of a girl student called Esther Cheshire. The warden of Africa Hall, where Esther had lodged, was called to give evidence. It was known that the warden, Mrs. Theresa Bukenya, was a courageous person of the highest integrity and that she intended to tell the commission everything she knew. The day before she was due to give evidence, on the 23rd June, three men called at Mrs. Bukenya's office on the campus. She was never seen again alive. The next day her body and the foetus of a child – she was eight months pregnant – were found floating in the river. She had been shot through the neck – a way of death favoured by the State Research Bureau.

When the students returned after the vacation at the beginning of last month they demanded to know the findings of Professor Langland's commission and to be given an explanation of Mrs. Bukenya's death. Information, they were told, was not available. It was then that they had begun to draw up a list of grievances to be presented in a petition to the Vice-Chancellor. These ranged from the comparatively trivial – the closing of the library at 6.00 p.m. instead of 11.00 p.m. due to a shortage of light-bulbs – to the more serious – lack of food – to the unacceptable – the presence of Amin's killers on the campus to keep an eye on the students.

Finally there were the complaints against Amin's son Taban who had recently been enrolled as a student in the engineering faculty and now had the run of the University. Taban's previous education was non-existent. He had worked for a time as a bicycle mechanic at Jinja, on the strength of which Amin had sent him to Russia to be trained as an aircraft engineer. After less than two months the Russians had sent him home to Uganda as unteachable. Two weeks ago Taban had transferred from engineering to the linguistics faculty and moved into a luxury flat on the campus, where he enjoyed special privileges and had his own food brought in from outside while other students went hungry. Accompanied everywhere by his bodyguards he came to classes with a pistol in his belt and a sub-machine gun under his arm. No-one dared to oppose him, even when he began going at night to the women's halls of residence, firing off his pistols in the dormitories, calling out any girl who took his fancy and then raping or beating her at gunpoint.

At this stage in his account the speaker paused. A soft breeze blew across the square and suddenly the audience became restless as if galvanised by hatred at the very mention of Taban's name. Most of them already knew the facts, if not at first hand, then from the pamphlets which had been distributed earlier in the proceedings, but to hear the truth spoken aloud, to take part in this open meeting which all of them knew was fraught with danger, gave them a feeling of solidarity and strength. As patriots they had long ago decided to lay down their lives if necessary for their country.

'The Vice-Chancellor will not accept our petition,' the speaker resumed, raising his voice now for the first time. 'He is a frightened man. We will go to State House ourselves and present it to Amin in person. They will try to stop us as they did once before. This time there may be bloodshed. Are you willing to take the chance?'

The crowd answered with a single concerted cry of 'Uhuru.' Then raising both arms in the air they began to sway and chant, calling out in cadenced slogans: 'Down with Amin. Down with his murderous dogs. Taban to the rubbish heap. We will not be slaves.'

In the corner of the square, standing in the shadow of an open doorway, as yet unnoticed by the chanting students, two officers of the Ugandan Army were observing the meeting. One of them, wearing steel-rimmed 'girl-watcher' sunglasses under his forage cap, turned and made a signal to someone inside the building.

Taking a short cut through Lumumba Hall, Michael Kinkasa arrived on the scene at the very moment the troops moved into the square. He was too late. Instinctively he ducked back into the safety of the hall as the soldiers ran by outside. He counted at least thirty-five, all from Uganda's most feared regiment, the Para-Commando Marine Unit. As Michael looked on in horror the soldiers, dressed in camouflage fatigues and with automatic weapons at the ready, quickly encircled the square at the upper level and took up position so that from every side their guns were trained down on the heads of the crowd.

The chanting stopped at once and the students, taken aback by the suddenness of the manoeuvre, made no move. The two officers stepped out of the shadows and slowly approached the young bearded man who had been doing all the talking. Three students from the crowd tried to climb up on the bank to give him support, but they were shoved back by the military. The speaker stood his ground, waiting until the officers came up to him: then he turned and shouted between cupped hands:

'Soldiers of Uganda! We are Ugandans too. We are patriots. We will surrender our lives willingly for Uganda. Join us in the struggle to overthrow the murderer, the tyrant Amin. . . .'

At that moment the officer standing closest to him drew his pistol and whipped it across the back of the student's head. He fell forward and rolled down the bank into the crowd. Watching from behind a curtained window of Lumumba Hall, Michael summoned his courage. Although as a junior lecturer he knew he could have little influence, he was on the point of stepping out to protest at the soldier's brutality when he noticed a gaily coloured Pepsi-Cola van move up into the approach road to the square and execute a half-turn which effectively blocked the only exit. As the students began to realise what was happening and saw that they had been trapped for a purpose, they began to run, converging on the steps and clambering the grassy banks in an attempt to reach the safety of the buildings. Only a few of them made it before the shooting started.

There was no word of command. The soldiers opened fire without warning, emptying their guns indiscriminately into the crowd. For a few seconds the rattle of automatic weapons echoed deafeningly about the close confines of the square. Then one of the officers shouted an order and as suddenly as it had begun the shooting stopped.

Michael's reactions to what was happening were slow. He had looked on in disbelief as the students were cut down, their bodies spun around by bullets, falling back from the slopes, blood jetting from magnified tracer wounds. He couldn't take in what he saw. It had happened too quickly. Now he found it difficult to tell the extent of the slaughter, how many had been killed or wounded. Some of the students had thrown themselves down on the ground as soon as the shooting started and were playing possum. He computed in a dazed, almost detached way that as many as fifty might have been hit badly, perhaps ten were dead.

The officer in the 'girl-watcher' sunglasses spoke through a loud hailer, ordering the students to lie face down on the ground with their hands behind their backs.

'This is bad behaviour,' his voice blared out across the square, 'bad against Uganda, bad against our President for Life, F.M. Amin.'

Abruptly, as if he had forgotten what he wanted to say next, he switched off the microphone and with an idle movement of the wrist signalled his troops down the slopes into the wailing crowd.

The beatings started and were carried out in a casual, almost haphazard way. The soldiers had shouldered their guns and wielding heavy sticks or drawn *pangas,* they sauntered among the prostrate bodies hitting or slashing at anything that drew their attention. It might be the colour of a shirt, a twisted limb or the manifestation of fear. There was no method to their selectivity. A wristwatch torn from a willing hand was paid for with blows. Insults might be ignored, a plea for mercy laughingly granted with the *panga.* Some were beaten so terribly that they would die later that afternoon of their wounds.

While the officers looked on with apparent approval, even amusement, the men did exactly as they pleased. Women were raped, their clothes torn from them or simply bundled up over their heads, while the soldiers took them one after another, usually from behind and standing up. Afterwards the girls were beaten. Any attempt to protect the women was dealt with most severely. One girl who tried to resist being raped was stripped naked by two soldiers and, while one of them held her arms, the other took her by the breasts and with a stroke of his *panga* severed each of them close to the chest. The soldiers counted this a great joke and when one of them asked if he might have them for his wife who was flat chested, the others all laughed uproariously, their high-pitched giggles running together horribly with the screams of the mortally wounded girl.

A small detachment of soldiers had moved into one of the halls of residence on the opposite side of the square to where Michael was hiding. Finding students in the dormitories they began throwing them from the third and fourth floor windows. Some were killed as they hit the ground, others broke bones and limbs and lay in awkward heaps where they fell. Shortly afterwards these soldiers reappeared, laughing, talking among themselves and smoking cigarettes. Forming up into a ragged column they waited for the others to finish their business on the square. One of the officers who seemed to have grown bored of the carry-on, blew three sharp notes on a whistle and the rest of the men, stopping only to button their trousers or deliver a last kick at the head or genitals of a prone student, trotted up to join the column. Then with a grinding of gears the Pepsi-Cola van was backed out of the approach road and the troops withdrew in order from their field of blood and butchery.

## THREE

In that short and terrible half-hour Michael had remained hidden behind a bark-cloth curtain in the recreation room of Lumumba Hall. As a silent witness to the massacre he felt pangs of remorse at doing nothing to try and prevent what happened. But it was not hard to persuade himself that this was no time to indulge feelings of guilt. Crossing himself, he went down on his knees and thanked God for sparing his life. Still numb with shock but, now that the soldiers had gone, beginning to shake with delayed reaction, he emerged cautiously from his hiding place. As fear left him he was overwhelmed suddenly by nausea. He fell on his knees again, retching till he thought his intestines would come up into his throat and suffocate him. He picked himself up and walked unsteadily out into the bright sunlit quadrangle of Freedom Square.

It was not what he had expected. In the short time he had been away from the window the soldiers had returned – perhaps they had never left – and were rounding up scores of students at gunpoint, herding them towards camouflaged Bedford trucks parked in the square. They took men and women, wounded and unscathed, anyone who was not quick enough to get away. But others, picking themselves up from their enforced prostration, saw what was going on and began a stampede towards the buildings. The dead and seriously wounded, red-gowned, white-shirted, spreadeagled on the grass like washing put out to dry in the sun, were trodden underfoot in the hurry to reach the relative safety of the halls of residence. The soldiers mostly let them go, finding it easier to handle those who were in no shape to run or offer resistance.

This time Michael felt compelled to act. He ran down the steps into the basin of the square, fighting his way through the crush of students coming the opposite way. He discovered the officer with the 'girl-watcher' sunglasses standing behind one of the lorries. He paused to catch his breath. Straightening his tie, he tried to assume a dignified and authoritative manner.

'What is the meaning of this?' he stammered. 'Where are you taking my students? I am Michael Chancellor . . . Michael Kinkasa, lecturer in English at Makerere and the Chancellor will want to know about this abominable outrage.'

The soldier looked up at him and laughed. 'The Chancellor himself has ordered that all unruly elements must be crushed.'

'These people need medical treatment. You must send for ambulances to take them to Mulago Hospital.'

'No-one is to leave the campus. Troops are guarding all entrances to prevent entering or leaving. I have orders that students should receive no treatment. Dispensary is closed for stock-taking. Go inside or you will all be killed like dogs.'

'Haven't you done that to us already? Where are you taking these students? Why do you want them? They have done nothing.,

'They are ringleaders.' The officer turned away. Michael

began to protest, but the strength of his disgust made him incoherent.

Without looking round the soldier said softly, 'Lecturer, lecturer, go away or it will be bad for you. University is for idiots and girls. This place is unnecessary to Uganda. What you have seen here is only the beginning. At Bugolobi we bury them with bulldozers, Lecturer in English, are you a ringleader?'

Michael saw the officer's head move a fraction. The sun caught the steel frame of his glasses. He took this as the final warning and in defeat moved away. He went back quickly along the walkway, picking his way between the groaning, blood-soaked bundles of humanity, shutting his ears to their cries for help, avoiding the eyes that rolled in supplication.

For the rest of that day and most of the coming night the wounded and dying and dead students lay where they had fallen. Anyone who tried to reach them to drag them back inside or give them medical assistance or merely a drink of water was signalled back by a soldier with a machine gun. Their continuous moaning and intermittent, agonised screams were heard all over the campus.

Inside the halls of residence the students had taken refuge in their dormitories. Barricading the doors with flimsy wardrobes and bed frames, they settled in to wait. Most of them shared out what little food they had, while some, not knowing what was to come, hoarded or ate secretively, causing resentment and bitterness. In Lumumba Hall, where more than two-thirds of the students were now missing, there was a half-hearted attempt at organising help from outside, but the only telephone was out of order and any movement on the campus was impossible. It was decided to do nothing until after dark.

The young bearded speaker of that morning's fateful meeting had turned up again at Lumumba. Recovered from the pistol whipping he had received from the officer, he had managed to avoid being beaten or rounded up by playing dead. Later, when the soldiers first left the square, he had crept back to the hall and safety. Taking him for a spokesman, Michael sought him out and asked him his views on what had happened.

'Taban must have 'phoned his father . . .' the student's eyes narrowed. 'He knew about the meeting beforehand. He had seen the petition and the complaints against him. He wanted to forestall, so to speak, to move against us before his crimes could come home to roost. Like father like son, totally predictable . . . but they know how to survive.'

'What we have just seen and lived through – the world must be told the truth,' Michael said earnestly.

'We're not through anything yet.'

There was an awkward pause. Michael fidgeted with his spectacles, then in a strangely formal gesture he put out his hand. 'My name is Kinkasa.'

'Tobias Mboya. Pleased to meet you. I've heard some things about you from your students.' He smiled and accepted the proffered hand. 'They say you're a fine lecturer on English poetry.'

'In a situation like this a degree in literature is not much use.'

'I am a medical student. I should be down there tending the wounded, but I am as helpless as you.' He looked down, as if embarrassed.

'They would shoot you,' Michael said warmly. 'I hardly know you, Tobias, nor do I know what will happen next, but I suspect there will be more need for you here than lying out in the square with a bullet through your brain.'

'What happens next depends on the whim of a devil. No sense now in our united front. We should think of saving our own skins.'

They were standing close to a window in one of the fourth floor domitories, watching for developments in the square below. Behind them the rows of empty cubicles, some with unmade beds and personal effects left lying about, were eloquent of their owners' absence.

It was after seven now and almost dark. As the tropical night came up, flooding the sky with sudden velvety blackness, the beam of a searchlight stabbed across the square and began to play from building to building. Shortly afterwards the campus 'street' lamps, which had been out of use for the last six months because of the 'need to conserve power,' came on all at once, drenching the University with unaccustomed light. The chances of getting off the campus now or even reaching one of the other buildings had been severely reduced.

Tobias turned away from the window. 'The soldiers are coming back, I know it. Tonight will see the worst.'

The second attack on Makerere came just before dawn on Wednesday, 4th August. At 3.00 a.m. President Amin's son, Taban, rode on to the campus at the head of two hundred of his father's troops, intent on taking his personal revenge on those who had tried to blacken his good name. 'Again there was terrific terror and butchery,' one of the students, who subsequently came out of Uganda, told a foreign journalist. 'More students were beaten and killed, more women raped and many of the wounded who had lain out on Freedom Square since the first attack were finished off with bayonets and *pangas.*'

This time the troops entered each of the halls of residence, ransacking the buildings and looting the students' property. They spent most of the time in the dormitories of Africa and Mary Stuart, the two women's halls. The pitiful screams of the girls, heard all over the campus, left no doubt about the nature of the atrocities that were committed there. After the soldiers left it was found that many of the women were missing. Others had been raped and abused so badly that they were unable to get up and walk. Later when they were carried to the dispensary on the campus, troops were standing by to prevent them from receiving treatment.

Michael saw the snub-nosed army trucks roll into the square and woke Tobias, who was sleeping fitfully in one of the cubicles. They had been taking it in turns to keep watch from the dormitory window. Now they acted swiftly according to a pre-arranged plan.

During the long hours of waiting Tobias had succeeded in cutting a neat manhole in the cardboard-thin ceiling of their dormitory. Climbing on to the back of a carefully balanced chair, then moving to a second footrest on the top of one of the iron cubicle frames, he pulled himself up effortlessly by a wooden beam and disappeared with a lizard-like movement into the ceiling cavity. Michael, who though taller was less athletic than Tobias, had more difficulty. In the dark, knocking over the chair – they had not dared turn on the light for fear of their window being marked – he reached up to save himself and succeeded only in tearing the edge of the hole, bringing down a shower of plaster on his head. There was no time to clear up, only to pull a blanket from one of the beds over the mess of white dust and hope that it would not attract notice. On the second attempt, with help from Tobias, Michael managed to scramble up into the roof.

Once inside he lay down as instructed along an uncomfortable length of wooden beam, taking care not to let any of his limbs rest on the cheap Kampala-made plasterboard. As soon as he was safely up, Tobias refitted the piece of ceiling he had cut away and fixed it back in place with a rather precarious arrangement of string. Then the two of them settled down to wait, wondering whether or not their makeshift trap-door was detectable from below. In a jerry-built student residence good hiding places were not easily found. Hopefully that meant the soldiers would not think of looking beyond the obvious ones.

Already they could hear them moving about on the floor below. There were the sounds of running footsteps, voices raised in anger, cries of protest, then a muffled but dreadful scream. It was cut short by the crash of broken glass, followed by brief silence – then a sickening thud.

Michael tried to swallow but his throat was too dry and his tongue stuck to the roof of his mouth. Afraid of choking in the airless, dust-filled atmosphere of the attic, he had to bite on his hand to keep down the irritation in his lungs. Sweat poured off his face and stung his eyes. Beside him he could hear Tobias moving restlessly and moaning gently to himself. He whispered to him to be quiet and the moaning stopped. Then he heard a different sound: a soft rustling noise coming out of the impenetrable darkness that lay ahead of them. As he realised the significance of that minute indication of movement, a new fear clutched at Michael's heart.

Below them doors banged open and shut along the corridors. Then came the heavy tramp of feet. Suddenly the noise was much closer. The soldiers had reached the top floor. He could hear them in the next dormitory, talking and laughing boisterously as they rifled through the students' lockers. Michael prayed for them to be quick, counting the seconds, pressing his wristwatch to his ear, partly to block out the knowledge of that other sound; but the rustling noise, a dry scraping along the top surface of the plasterboard, would not go away. Not daring to move he held his breath and bit deeper into his hand.

After an eternity the door burst open and the soldiers clattered into the dormitory. Snapping on the lights, they set to work on their systematic search of the cubicles. Through the circular crack surrounding their trap door, slightly enlarged where Michael had torn its edge, light seeped into the attic space revealing Tobias's outstretched hands holding the string which kept the board in place. Cautiously lifting his head Michael stared ahead of him, trying to see beyond that small area of illumination. The soldiers in the room below were forgotten as he followed the line of the wooden beam on which he lay and strained his eyes into the darkness. To the right of the joist he thought he detected a faint movement. Again, only this time quite clearly, he saw something that gleamed. An eye, a slither of tongue darting between dry jaws, then the square flat head and behind it the thick coils of a puff adder. The snake was advancing slowly towards him, its head not a yard away from his face.

With a stifled yell Michael pulled himself back and rolled sideways in a single fluid movement. As he transferred his full weight on to the plasterboard, the ceiling gave beneath him. Clutching at his companion he brought Tobias with him and the two of them crashed down on to the floor below.

The soldiers, taken by surprise, nevertheless reacted swiftly. Dazed from the fall, Michael saw, as if in slow motion, a rifle butt swing down in a leisurely arc over Tobias's head before the lights exploded between his own eyes and darkness closed in all round.

# FOUR

At first, when they realised that they were not being taken to Makindye Prison or Naguru Barracks, the infamous headquarters of the Public Safety Unit, there was momentary relief among the students in the back of the three-ton Bedford. But few had hopes of a kinder fate. It was simply preferable to be left in uncertainty, not to know where they were bound or exactly what was going to happen to them – though that did not stop them from trying to find out. With the canvas flaps down and soldiers who answered no questions sitting to the rear, there was no way of taking bearings. But it soon became clear from the length of time they had been in motion that they had left Kampala far behind. Someone suggested that they might be on the Jinja road. They had been travelling straight and at high speeds and were still meeting a few cars coming the other way. Then the truck slowed and made a sharp left turn, leaving the tarmac surface for a rough *murrum* track. Now they were on their own. For an hour or more they were tossed about in the back of the lorry, constantly being thrown off balance and on to the wounded who lay on the floor and groaned at every jolt.

Michael came to with a rush of pain to the head. At first he thought he was alone and felt sudden panic at finding himself in the dark. There was an unbearable roaring in his ears and the smell of diesel oil and vomit made his gorge rise. His face rested on something warm and sticky that moved under him. The contact reminded him of some ineffable horror and he tried to pull away, only to find that one of his hands was trapped. There were weights tied to his legs. He heard voices. So at least he was not alone. His head pounded with each consecutive stroke of returning consciousness. The roaring in his ears resolved itself into the throb of a heavy-duty lorry engine.

'Michael, are you all right? Michael, it's me, Tobias. Are you hurt?'

The voice was close to his head. A hand gripped his shoulder. Relief flooded over him. He was not alone. He tried to move again, the pain concentrated in his fingers.

'It was the snake, Tobias,' he heard himself say. 'I'm sorry.'

'That's all right. They'd probably have found us anyway.'

'A bloody great puff adder. I can't stand snakes . . . what about you?'

'I'm O.K. Don't talk. Conserve your strength.'

The truck lurched and Michael's hand came free. All this time, he thought, someone has been standing on my hand. It was getting lighter and he could make out dim shapes. Then the truck slowed and ground to a halt. He heard voices outside and the sound of doors slamming. Presently the flap was rolled back and Michael caught a glimpse of dawn sky behind a fringe of tall trees. Then he saw the arc lamps and barbed wire.

The soldiers jumped down and with threats and curses began discharging the truck's cargo.

'A holiday camp in one of Uganda's famous nature reserves,' a student said facetiously. 'We are here courtesy of the "Gen." All expenses paid.'

'Now tell us the bad news,' said another.

As they were herded towards the compound there was laughter.

There was no shelter inside the compound and the two hundred or more students spent the next three days lying or squatting in an area roughly the size of a basket-ball pitch without water or food, waiting for the cool of evening – the only respite they could look forward to without fear. Hope of escape soon evaporated. The barbed wire palisades were well constructed and the guards, grim-faced peasants who belonged to Amin's own West Nile Kakwa tribe, were changed at regular intervals throughout the day and night. They were posted both inside and outside the compound. When they went off duty they retired to a guard hut on the edge of the forest two hundred yards from the compound. There were no other signs of life. The whirr of cicadas and the cries of birds and Columbus monkeys were the only sounds they heard.

At night the arc lamps attracted clouds of insects and usually one or two enormous moths from the forest which crashed repeatedly against the hot glass and sometimes knocked themselves out. If they fell inside the compound there was an ugly scramble to catch them. They were devoured immediately and the guards laughed at the prisoners' hunger.

On the second evening two of the students approached a guard and asked for something to eat, offering the promise of money to be paid when they got back to Kampala. While he considered the proposition the guard drew his *panga*, then stepping forward with a toothy grin took a powerful swipe at the throat of the student nearest to him. The blow almost decapitated the boy. He fell forwards with his head hanging by a hank of muscle half way down his back. The brief rasping soud of air escaping through his severed windpipe drew the attention of every prisoner in the compound. The guard knelt and with a second stroke chopped the head from the body. He stood up and facing the horrified students made a grinning display of licking the blood from the blade of his knife.

'If you are hungry, you can all eat,' he shouted at them and turned enquiringly to the second student, who was still standing beside him, too afraid to move away. Then, as if he could not think of what next to do for his audience, the guard lashed out again with his *panga*, missing the neck this time but laying open the side of the boy's face. He screamed and the guard, who seemed irritated by the noise, hit him again and went on chopping at his head and shoulders until he stopped screaming and fell down at his feet in a bloody pulp.

The other guards, who had been watching the performance with interest, threw a bucket over the compound wire and told one of the students to collect the blood from the body. Two more prisoners, with rifles held to their heads, were given knives and ordered to butcher the corpses. The flesh was then collected in a sack and taken away to be cooked over a fire. Later that night the guards came back with the roast meat and the bucket of blood. They had been drinking *waragi* – a Ugandan liquor made from bananas – and their mood was volatile. They picked students at random and tried to make them eat and drink. Those who refused were forced to swallow at gunpoint. Anyone who failed to control his stomach was shot. In due course their bodies were also cut up for meat.

The following day the killing began in earnest. At dawn the guards entered the compound and kicked the exhausted prisoners until they were awake and on their feet. They selected ten of the strongest looking men and marched them out of the compound to the edge of the forest clearing, where they were given spades and told to dig a shallow trench, perhaps fifteen feet long by four feet wide. In their weakened state it took them most of the day to complete the task. When it was done they were ordered to stand in a row alongside what none of them doubted was to become their grave. Ten more prisoners were then brought out from the compound and after being supplied with hammers were ordered to stand close behind the trench diggers. On the word of command they were to beat in the brains of the person standing in front of them.

The first time the order was given nobody moved. The soldiers lifted their guns to their shoulders. The order was repeated. This time several hammers were falteringly raised. The prisoners watching from the compound, standing up against the wire, turned their heads away. One hammer came down. But by now the soldiers had grown impatient and without waiting for a command they began shooting. The bodies pitched forward into the trench. One man tried to run, but was picked off before he reached the trees. When they stopped firing, the soldiers walked forward to the trench and kicked some of the bodies that had fallen the wrong way back into the hole. Then ten more students were called out to fill in the trench with earth. Afterwards they were shot or beaten to death by the soldiers and their bodies left lying where they fell.

That night the soldiers drank more heavily than usual.

It was a quarter to one by Michael's wristwatch – typically enough the guards had not bothered to search them for valuables – when the soldiers left the guardhouse and came staggering over to the compound, their uniforms undone, some barely able to stand, but all carrying weapons. He looked at Tobias, who was lying beside him staring up at the stars, a resigned, almost peaceful expression on his face. Suddenly Michael felt certain that they were going to die. During the past three days they had survived by not attracting attention to themselves, by taking care never to catch the eye of a guard, but also never to be caught trying to avoid it. Now, he thought, as he watched the platoon of drunken Kakwa approach, their efforts to stay alive had been wasted. After tonight there would be no survivors.

Michael prayed, no longer for sustenance, but for forgiveness. He imagined himself kneeling at the altar rail of Rubaga Cathedral where as a child he had once knelt to receive his first communion. The filth and gruesome squalor of his surroundings, the warm intestinal smell of death and putrefaction fell away. He thought of Ruth, the girl he had loved, and the better times they had known together. He relived memories of happiness in his family circle, at home in Ntemkoge, his ancestral village, and he remembered a time when he had been full of hope for the future of his country. He asked for forgiveness for his refusal to recognise the truth of what had happened since then. Perhaps one day, he thought, God would come back to Uganda.

Tobias touched his arm. 'I've had an idea,' he said, 'that might just save us.'

The soldiers had reached the gate to the compound and were fumbling with the lock, laughing and cursing at the difficulty they were having in getting it open. Some of them were already unshouldering their weapons and carelessly testing bolt actions and firing mechanisms. The prisoners, galvanised by those harsh, metallic sounds which had become all too familiar to them in the past few days, rose to their feet and began backing away from the entrance. No-one doubted that there was to be slaughter.

As the soldiers kicked open the gate and advanced into the middle of the compound, the students began to run in search of non-existent cover. Some lay down and hugged the dirt, others pushed themselves back against the wire or tried to climb it. Others came forward on their knees and pleaded for mercy. Michael and Tobias, taking advantage of the confusion, walked calmly to the far end of the compound.

Since the first killings inside the wire, the prisoners had mostly kept to the other end, leaving this corner to a heap of bodies which the guards had deliberately left unburied. To show some respect for their former colleagues, the students had stacked their bodies in a neat pile, using their clothes to cover it over. The funeral mound, which had been added to at regular intervals, stood nearly three feet high. During the day it buzzed with flies and vermin and gave off a stench that hung over the whole camp.

Michael and Tobias lay down behind the mound on the side closest to the fence and quickly pulled off some of their clothes. Stretched out on the ground, they covered their heads and joined themselves to that grim stinking pile, literally embracing death.

Once the shooting started it did not let up. Michael saw nothing. He heard only the screams, the long bursts of automatic fire as one weapon then another took up the monotonous theme, and the thump of falling bodies. Some dropped near where they lay and even on top of them. Michael was grateful for the extra cover they afforded. He hoped only that the guards would wait until morning to dispose of the corpses.

The firing stopped. The echoes persisted briefly in his ears, then followed a terrible silence. He found himself listening for some sign of life, hoping despite himself that there were no survivors to give the soldiers the idea of checking their handiwork. But there was only the sound of their voices, chattering among themselves in Kakwa and laughing as they left the compound and retreated towards the guard hut to celebrate their victory, no doubt, with another bottle of *warugi*. He wondered if they had bothered to lock the gates of the compound. Then, miraculously, the arc lamps overhead were extinguished.

In the dark he felt it safe to make a move, but Tobias whispered to him to wait. They waited. Five minutes became ten. Nothing stirred. Cautiously, making no sound, they drew free from the tangled corpses and stood up. They could see very little. An oil light outside the guardhouse two hundred yards away gave them a bearing, no more.

As they moved slowly towards the gate of the compound, they had to pick their way by touch, using their feet as antennae, between the corpses. In places the ground was so well covered with bodies that it was impossible to avoid standing on them. Here and there they could hear breathing and a low whimpering. They blocked their ears to the sound. Once, as Michael stepped on something soft and pliant, a terrible groan rose from the ground. To cover a distance of not more than twenty yards, it took them as many minutes: it was a journey they would remember for the rest of their lives.

They found the gate open and unguarded. As they passed through, Michael crossed himself and offered thanks to God, but neither he nor Tobias felt any release. With an unspoken farewell to those they were leaving behind, they walked away stealthily in the direction of the trees.

## FIVE

The sun rose over the escarpment, brightening the dark, broad sweep of river where it curved between banks edged with gallery forest. In the distance behind the fringe of acacias, the deep-throated roaring of lions, moving through open savanna looking for a place to lie up after gorging themselves on the night's kill, was taken up from the river by the friendly grunting of a herd of hippos. A fish eagle perching high on a dead *iroko* tree took off and flapped its leisurely way down stream. Hammerkops and spurwing plovers dipped and splashed over turgid backwaters. The rays of the sun grew stronger, bringing warmth and with it the renewal of life in all its tropical profusion to the riverbank.

Long dark shapes like floating logs, grounded in the mirror stillness of the shallows, began to move closer to the shore. Presently an armour-plated back rose silently from the water, then the long snout and tapering saw-tooth tail, as the crocodile slithered up quickly on to the sandy shelving bank and flopped down on its belly. It was followed by a second and then a third and within half an hour at least twenty of the massive reptiles lay basking in the sun, restoring body heat lost during the long night in the river.

From a bed of reeds, perhaps thirty yards from where the crocodiles lay, Michael and Tobias kept watch. Nearby a cart track led down to the water's edge. It had been used recently by heavy vehicles, and now that they were so near to their goal they were taking no chances. Once across the river, according to Tobias's calculations, it was less than thirty miles to the Kenyan border.

They had spent the night in the forest after collapsing at the foot of a tree, too exhausted to hide or even take basic precautions against wild animals. At dawn they had started walking due east and had been surprised to come to the river so soon. Although they had overheard the guards talking about getting their water from its banks, they had been prepared for a hike of several miles. After their initial joy, gratefully drinking their fill and washing the blood and dirt from their clothes, the question that preoccupied them now was how to get across. There was no sign of a boat or raft or even a suitable log on which they might have floated downstream, risking the crocodiles. They had the choice of either waiting till dark and following the river south until they came to a village – where there might be a chance of stealing a canoe – or swimming for it. Both alternatives seemed fraught with danger. For the time being they decided to stay where they were and rest up.

Some time after midday the drowsy peace of the riverside was disturbed by the roar of an approaching engine. Birds flew up from the water's edge and small shore animals made for cover, while one by one the great saurians slipped back into the shallows and sank out of sight. Michael and Tobias, who had both been dozing in spite of their agreement that one of them should keep watch at all times, woke with a start. Looking out over the tops of the reeds Michael saw a Bedford army lorry, perhaps two hundred yards away, coming down the cart track towards the river. At that moment a slight disturbance on the bank behind them made him look round. He was just in time to see a dishevelled figure covered in blood from head to foot, eyes wild with pain and fright, jumped down into the reeds beside them.

The man lay where he had fallen, one arm twisted up

behind his back. After they had recovered their wits, Michael and Tobias helped him to sit up. He had been wounded in the shoulder and was bleeding heavily. They signalled to him to keep quiet, but the man insisted on trying to speak and in a hoarse, feverish whisper began to explain how he had escaped that morning from the camp – when, to their profound relief, he fainted.

The army truck had come to a halt a few yards from the river bank. Two soldiers jumped down from the cab and with a lot of shouting helped the driver to execute a three-point turn. Then the vehicle was reversed almost to the water's edge, so that it tilted at an angle down towards the river. The soldiers undid the canvas flaps and released the fastenings to the rear end. At once a great jumble of bodies poured out of the truck on to the sand, a few spilling over into the water. One of the soldiers then climbed into the back and kicked out the few remaining stragglers. When he had finished, they closed up the rear and the two men, whistling merrily, as if they had just delivered a load of *matoke* or potatoes, swung themselves up into the cab. Then the truck drove off. The whole operation had taken not longer than five minutes.

After the sound of the engine had died away Michael turned to Tobias: 'Now what do we do? It was your idea to wait here. Look at that!' – he pointed disdainfully at their new companion – 'What do we do about him?'

'We take him with us,' said Tobias quietly.

'You must be mad. We should leave here now, without him. He'll only hold us back. This is exactly what I was afraid of . . .'

The man opened his eyes and sat up, looking around him in bewilderment. Then, as if he had remembered that the bad dream was nothing but reality, the haunted look returned to his eyes. He struggled to get up, but the others held him.

'They're coming through the forest. They saw me get away,' he babbled. 'They'll find us here and kill us all.'

Michael looked at Tobias with a certain grim satisfaction. 'That means, if this fellow is right, that it's time to go. We shall have to swim for it.'

'Actually, now is not a bad time,' said Tobias. 'After that

last delivery the crocs are going to be too busy to bother with us.' He turned to the third man: 'Can you swim with that arm?' The man said nothing but nodded repeatedly.

As they made their way down to the water's edge, Michael looked back to the sandbank where the bodies had been dumped. The crocodiles had returned and in greater numbers than before. Already most of the corpses that had fallen into the water had disappeared. He saw one floater suddenly tugged at from under the surface and pulled down into the depths. Up on the bank one of the brutes had dragged a body from the pile and was moving around the carcass with a leg between its jaws, trying to twist the limb off at the socket.

' "Nature's scavengers," my biology master used to call them.'

'Amin's sanitation corps,' said Tobias, as they waded out cautiously into the warm muddy water.

They began to swim, trying to keep upstream on the principle that the nearer they stayed to where the crocodiles were feeding the more likely they were to be ignored, but the current was too strong and carried them quickly down river. In the water the river appeared much wider than it had from the shore and the opposite bank remained impossibly far away. Michael felt his strength ebbing fast and began to doubt whether he could last the course. But after all they had come through the prospect of drowning now seemed to him an ignominious end and his determination to survive was reinforced. He struck out with renewed vigour.

The three of them had started off swimming in close formation, but now as they passed the middle of the stream the gap between them widened. Inevitably, Michael and Tobias were doing better than their handicapped companion, who had been carried thirty yards or more downstream from them. But he was still making headway. Tobias shouted to him to keep going. They were drawing closer at last to the far bank.

Michael swam on, concentrating only on reaching the bank, keeping his eyes fixed on a strip of yellow sand between two thickets of papyrus. He had persuaded himself that the sand there was pure gold and that beyond the fringe of silver palm trees lay the most beautiful land in the world.

Then, moving out quietly from behind the reeds, he saw the crocodile. It came waddling across the sandpit and slid down an incline into the river, the water seething over its broad scaly back. Michael watched in horror as fully twenty-two feet of vicious, predatory reptile vanished beneath the surface.

'Crocodile!' he screamed at Tobias.

'Keep swimming,' the reply came back. 'Swim for your life.'

Michael swam with sick fear spreading from his groin to the extremities of every apprehensive limb. He tried to fix his eyes again on the strip of sand, but found it impossible to concentrate. Constantly scanning the water all around him, a moment later he saw the crocodile again, only its eyes showing above the surface, twin black periscopes that suddenly hooded over with a glistening yellowish membrane. As it winked it raised its head a fraction in the water, revealing an expanse of hard scaly skin and the gleaming white points of two tusk-like teeth that pushed up from the lower jaw into the constriction of its snout.

The crocodile was floating downstream half way between the two friends and the other man. Tobias urged them on, shouting as loudly as he could to frighten the beast off, when it submerged for the second time. They were within ten yards of the bank, almost there – dry land, safety. Michael felt his knees touch the bottom and found that he could stand. Then, as he staggered ashore at last, he heard a dreadful cry. Looking back he saw the massive saurian shoot up from under the surface in a wild swirl of foam and spray, its bright orange jaws opening wide for a moment before it seized its prey about the middle and, holding him clamped between interlocking teeth, swung round in the boiling water and with a great splash and swish of its tail vanished beneath the surface.

A moment later Tobias came up beside him and, pulling each other from the water, they clambered up on to the high bank of the river, out of danger's reach, and threw themselves down on to the sandy ground, trembling with shock and exhaustion, but alive.

Michael Kinkasa and Tobias Mboya escaped across the

Ugandan border into Kenya on the 10th August, 1976, one week after the soldiers moved on to the campus at Makerere University. In Nairobi they stayed at the home of Michael's uncle, who had heard of the trouble at Makerere through the official news bulletins of Radio Kampala. Aware of the real nature of conditions in Uganda, he had found the reports extremely worrying and had tried to get in touch with Michael by telephone, only to be told that all lines to Makerere were out of order.

One of the Kampala Radio bulletins had been reproduced in a Kenyan newspaper. He showed it to Michael and Tobias, who read the clipping with interest.

'Today [4th August] police arrested a small number of students at Makerere University. These students had been causing trouble on the campus and spreading false rumours. According to a military spokesman, President Amin, who was attending the colourful and jubilant celebrations of Uganda's recent successes in the "economic war," later issued a warning against rumour-mongering and urged people always to listen to UBC and read the *Voice of Uganda* for correct and up-to-date information. Field Marshal Amin said that these people are nothing but first-class liars and likewise they are notoriously known as international confusing elements.

'As Chancellor of the University he reminded students at Makerere that they must study hard and live cleanly. The President for Life said that he liked the students very much but that he had a couple of rockets for them. He said Uganda is not a slave camp, as the Imperialists and Zionists have been saying, but an independent nation of freedom, liberty and justice. F.M. Amin also made it clear that, being a military leader, whatever he says must be taken very seriously because he is not joking, like most politicians. He can act, once the situation demands . . .'

With money borrowed from his uncle. Michael left Nairobi with Tobias towards the end of August and came to Britain. Tobias, as a supporter of Milton Obote and the Uganda People's Congress, wanted to go to Tanzania to join other socialist Ugandan exiles in working towards building their country's future, but Michael had persuaded him that he would be able to achieve more from London.

In the days they had spent kicking their heels in Nairobi, brooding over their recent experiences and drinking too much Nile beer, Michael had reached the conclusion that he had been given a mission to fulfil. He, too, could act, he decided, once the situation demanded. And now it demanded: above all else in life, he wanted revenge.

## *Part Two*

# OPERATION HIPPO

## ONE

*February 1977, London*
The curtains were half drawn, arranged to let in a strip of winter-grey sky and give a sectional view across the river of the dismal collection of buildings along the Embankment. Under the window on a wide double bed, made up with carefully rumpled pale satin sheets and a jumble of heart-shaped pillows, lay a beautiful black girl in cream satin de lys pyjamas.

Contrast. Out there cold ugly reality – the depressing world of crisis Britain; inside – warmth, elegance, tropical promise.

The girl was reclining with one leg tucked under her so that it pushed forward her pelvis, a slim arm thrown back behind her head in a gesture of abandonment. The thin straps of her camisole slid provocatively off her shoulders and the fringe of lace across her high, full breasts was drawn tight, allowing the merest suggestion of dark circles of skin beneath the petit point. She was gazing up at a man, whose shadow fell across the lower part of her body. Her brown, almond-shaped eyes were soft and eager with desire; the full, moist, pagoda-red lips slightly parted so that they glistened alluringly under the lights. She might have been asking him to make love to her, begging him to take her . . . now, this very instant.

There was a whirr of shutter clicks. "Fantastic, Ruth, darling!' the man enthused in weary professional tones. 'Absolutely fantastic. I just want you to try it once more, only this time I want you to think – remember what I said – *Think SATIN!*'

The girl looked down at her chest and said nothing. Then with a languid movement of her long, supple limbs she sat up and, slipping from the bed, set out towards the door of the changing room.

'Ruth, darling, where do you think you're going?'

'That's it, Maurice. You got your pictures. I'm tired now and I have to stop. My boyfriend is waiting for me down in the lobby. He is taking me flying again. You know, I'm getting pretty expert now. See you.'

She gave a little wave and walked off the studio floor, moving as gracefully as a Thomson's gazelle and leaving the photographer standing beside a fake palm tree with one petulant wrist bent on his hip and a rather sour expression on his face. He handed the Nikkormat to his assistant, who immediately began to rewind the film, an eager and grateful apprentice. The door of the changing room banged shut.

'Let me tell you something, Roger. African girls are the worst. They're late, they're lazy, they're temperamental. What's more they *all* think they're God's gift to . . . Coming on like the bloody Queen of Sheba.'

'You got some great shots, Maurice.'

'Stupid black bitch . . .'

Roger looked horrified. 'She can hear.'

In the changing room Ruth smiled to herself and gave a sigh of relief as she stepped out of the satin pyjamas and quickly began wiping off her make-up. Maurice was no worse than the others. Modelling, photographic sessions, fashion – she loathed the whole silly business. But at least it paid the bills. The money was good and it gave her some satisfaction to be earning more than the others – more than all of them put together. Sometimes she despaired of them, 'the friends', as they had recently decided to call themselves. They really were a hopeless bunch, but she needed them. In one very real sense they were all she had. She put them from her mind as she got back into her own clothes, pulling on an old pair of jeans, a big woolly Shetland sweater and her 'flying' boots.

She was looking forward to this afternoon. First lunch at The Old Bell, Hurley, and then on to the tiny airfield outside Oxford, where Julian kept his plane. They would drink Pimms and have roast beef and Julian would talk about his wife and children. It was the one thing that irritated her about him, but it was not really important. The flying was what mattered.

The first time he'd taken her up in the Cessna, she'd nearly died with excitement and later, when he had let her take the controls, she'd simply fallen in love – not so much with Julian as with the air, with flying. After he began giving her lessons, of course, they'd started sleeping together, but only on an occasional basis. It was not really a love affair between them, more a case of friendship. She suspected that the sex didn't mean much more to him than it did to her. She had other men in her life and he had his family and other interests – mostly to do with making money. But he enjoyed her company and felt flattered by her shared enthusiasm for flying. For her part she looked forward to going solo next week and then perhaps to getting her pilot's licence in the spring. In anticipation of that day she had bought an old flying jacket from Laurence Corner and stitched on a pair of R.A.F. 'wings.' But then 'the friends' had pointed out to her that wearing decorations without due entitlement was worthy of the Hippo and she had been forced to take them off. They were right, of course, but it was typical of them to be so serious about a little thing.

Ruth picked up the wing-less jacket and went to the window. Julian's car, a silver-grey Porsche, was parked in the street below. That's what they objected to, she thought. But why shouldn't she enjoy the good life? It didn't mean she was any less devoted to the cause. Hadn't she suffered, too? So what gave them the right to tell her how to be? It also meant she had a better cover than any of them could come up with. She tossed her head in annoyance and reached for the door to the studio.

It opened before her. Maurice was there, offering a telephone. 'For you,' he said, 'but in future, Ruth, darling, don't give them my number, there's a sweet thing.'

She took the receiver from him, letting him hold the cradle. The voice in her ear, a soft African accent that was instantly familiar, made her heart sink.

'A few friends are meeting for a drink at The Old Swan, Vicarage Crescent, in about half an hour . . .'

'You know I can't,' she interrupted quickly, forcing a smile for Maurice's benefit. 'Friday is my day for flying – I told you. Julian's here already. We were just leaving.'

The voice in her ear, softer still, said 'Only a drink or so. The pub is on the river not very far from the studio. Just follow the main road. You can't miss it. The friends would be a little bit disappointed not to see you.'

Ruth recognised the agreed procedure for calling an urgent meeting. 'All right, I'll be there,' she said and put the receiver down. For a second or two she stared at the telephone, trying to control her irritation and at the same time doing some quick thinking.

'Maurice, darling,' she murmured, looking up sweetly at the photographer. 'I know I'm asking a big favour, but you see I've got this African boy and he really is the jealous type. I'm afraid I'm going to have to stand up Julian. So be an angel, won't you, and pop down and tell him I'm sick or something. I think I'd better slip out the back way. If those two meet up there might be fireworks.'

Maurice stared at her in disbelief as she leant forward from the waist and kissed him lightly on the cheek. Then, swinging her flying jacket over one shoulder, Ruth walked across the studio and disappeared through the door marked EXIT.

'Oh, shit,' said the photographer.

The choice of The Old Swan as a meeting place was thought to be a reasonable one. The clientele being racially mixed at lunchtime, their presence would not attract undue attention, and the 'Lighterman Bar,' a comfortable lounge with large windows giving a panoramic view of industrial riverscape (which Tobias found very impressive), was busy enough to drown most conversation. None of them had been there before and it was far enough away from their usual haunts to make a chance encounter with someone they knew unlikely. In the past few weeks the friends had begun taking extra precautions. They avoided the places now which Ugandans and other Africans living in London were known to frequent and had agreed never to use the same pub twice. Arrangements for meetings were always made at the last minute, which sometimes created difficulties, but was considered worth the inconvenience.

Michael Kinkasa had secured a table by one of the windows overlooking the river. Reserving four places with his coat and briefcase, he sat watching Tobias make his way back from the crush at the bar, carrying two half pints of Carlsberg lager. He smiled encouragingly at him, amused by the younger man's determination not to spill a drop and still impressed by the easy way in which Tobias had adapted himself to London life – or at least certain aspects of it. He had never been out of Uganda before and at first had been slightly bewildered. Since October he had suffered terribly – as they all did to begin with – from the cold, but in the 'British Pub' Tobias had at once found his spiritual home. Whereas Michael and the others did not care much for drinking and used to meet in pubs only because they were convenient and cheap, for Tobias it was a serious pleasure, spoilt only by their straitened circumstances.

'Osaya, I suppose, is going to be late,' he said, setting down the drinks. 'What's his excuse this time?'

'Like all Langi he doesn't have what you call a sense of timing.' Michael laughed.

'You mean he's with that girl again. Even during the lunch break they're at it hammer and tongs. She's a bad influence for him. In Uganda before the exodus there were white girls like her who were mad for sex with African boys. They ended badly.'

'Osaya might be a little infatuated, but he's solid.' Tobias had a puritan streak, which Michael put down to his Protestant upbringing as much as his political idealism. 'My only worry is that he wants to bring her into the group.'

'That's out of the question. I have to tell you I worry about Osaya sometimes. How much do we know about him? He tells us his father was killed in the Mutukula slaughter. He shows us a few scars which he says he got from his time in the punishment block at Makindye. Now, you know, no-one comes out of that place so easily. How should we believe him when the next thing after being released from prison he is sent to London on an engineering course?'

'That was in '73. Things in Uganda were not so bad then.'

'How do you know? You weren't even there.' Tobias was in an excitable mood and ready to pick a fight. 'Even last summer you refused to admit what was going on – like the three bloody monkeys. You said so yourself.'

'Oh, I'm not disguising that fact. But what help is it to sow discord among the friends? You'll put us all in jeopardy with your suspicious thoughts.'

'But what if Osaya is one of Amin's people, planted on us for spying?'

'When he says he has reason to hate that man, I believe him.'

'Just the same way you believe Ruth and her stories of persecution. If those two were serious about it, would they spend their time playing football and screwing white girls like Osaya, or being a rich man's playgirl . . .?' Tobias stopped short, realising that he had gone too far.

Michael said nothing and looked down at his beer. He pushed back his gold-rimmed spectacles, which had a habit of falling forward over the flat bridge of his nose. One of the lenses had been cracked during their escape from the forest prison camp and he had not bothered to have it fixed.

'I'm sorry,' Tobias said. 'That was hitting below the belt.'

'It's all right,' Michael smiled. 'She may be a bit of a gadabout, but she's never let us down or missed a meeting . . ."

'Speaking of the devil.' Tobias laughed.

Ruth Utegi, turning heads as she went, picked her way through the crowded bar towards the two friends in the window. Despite his vow not to let the past interfere with their present commitment, Michael watched her progress with a mixture of admiration and resentment.

'So, I made it,' she said throwing her flying jacket down on the corner seat beside them, and herself into a separate chair. Still angry at having to break her flying date, Ruth's own feelings at the sight of her fellow countrymen, in their quiet suits and thin unstylish ties nursing their half pints of lager, were equally mixed. 'It's been a shocking morning. I could do with a drink, please. I'll have a scotch and ginger ale.'

The two men looked at her. Ruth waited, then making a

pretence of remembering, dipped into her enormous handbag and after rummaging about produced the money with a little flourish that was intended to humiliate.

'Tobias, be a darling,' she said gaily, handing him a five-pound note. 'With lots of ice.'

Younger, less sophisticated and of humbler stock than Michael or Ruth, Tobias was unused to women behaving in this way, and he went off to get the drink with a deliberate show of bad grace.

'That boy is a peasant,' Ruth said grandly as soon as he was out of earshot then, lowering her voice and leaning towards Michael, she whispered dramatically: 'Well, what's happening? Don't tell me someone's come up with another brilliant idea?'

'As a matter of fact, I have.'

'Like the one for bribing an official at Lancaster House to leave a drawing pin dipped in curare on his conference chair? I've got a suggestion. What about concealing a snake in some bagpipes and sending it to him as a gift from the Scottish Nationalists?'

'Very funny, but that's precisely why I called this meeting. It's not the time for joking any more. When the others come I'll tell you what it's about.'

They talked, not very successfully, about other things. Except when they were discussing the project, Michael and Ruth could say little to each other that did not end in bitterness or recrimination. Although it was nearly a year now since they had broken up, shortly before he returned to Uganda to take up the teaching post at Makerere, the scars had not healed. They were somewhat relieved, therefore, when Tobias returned with Ruth's whisky and three more lagers.

Close behind him came Osaya Nagere, the fourth and last friend. A stocky, powerfully built man in his late thirties, he was darker skinned than the others and had more pronounced negroid features. Snappily dressed in a loud check sportscoat, with flared claret trousers and a pair of multi-coloured platform shoes, he had a cheerful open face that made Tobias's suggestion that he might be a spy seem a little far-fetched. Apologising for being late, he rounded off a list of blatant excuses with a gale of high-pitched laughter that the others found quite infectious.

The joking and gossiping about friends, rumours and general goings on both here and in Uganda continued for rather too long. Finally Michael convened the meeting and though anyone observing the party of Africans in the window of the Lighterman Bar would not have noticed much change in their behaviour, they settled down to serious discussion.

'I called this meeting,' Michael addressed the others, 'and on an urgent basis, because I have a proposition to make. So far, you'll agree, we have achieved almost nothing. It is the end of February now and if he comes, that means three months in which to prepare ourselves for the attempt. All we have so far are a lot of madcap suggestions that couldn't possibly work. In fact this whole project is in danger of becoming a farce.'

'I am going to disagree quite heartily.' Osaya leant forward and put a square fist down in the middle of the table. 'I think one or two of our schemes could come off.'

Of the four Osaya was considered the most experienced, the practical one, the man of action, and Michael had brought him into the group for that reason. He had served for a short time in the Ugandan Army before Amin came to power and was the only one of them who knew how to handle a gun. Although he did not possess a weapon of any description, it was generally understood that Osaya would be the chief executive of what they had christened 'Operation Hippo.' After seeing the film 'Raid on Entebbe' at the Odeon, Tottenham Court Road, Osaya had been assigned the duties of military commander, and when Ruth had suggested giving him the code name 'Charles Bronson,' he had been more than delighted, though the idea hadn't quite caught on.

'An ambush on the M4 motorway, on his way in from Heathrow. One of us steals a lorry and jack-knifes it across the road in front of the cars, like this' – to illustrate his plan Osaya began moving empty glasses across the table – 'while the others are waiting behind a bank over here, with grenades and mortar bombs and . . .'

'That's totally absurd.' Tobias interrupted him: 'Where in God's name would we get mortar bombs? I think our original concept was the best – that each of us pursue his own plan, giving us four separate attempts in all. Our target has the luck of the devil. Look how many have failed. He has escaped every time, so that people at home seriously believe his life is charmed. But with four different attempts – one after the other, co-ordinated, and with shared responsibility and help for each other's plans where help is necessary – we cannot fail.'

'We haven't got one plan that's even vaguely realistic, let alone four.' Ruth made a clicking noise with her tongue and stared out of the window, wishing she was up there in the Cessna, free as a bird over the Oxford countryside.

'That's why I called this meeting.' Michael felt it was time now to intervene. He reached for the secondhand Samsonite briefcase that he had bought from the British Rail Lost Property Office and, opening it with two impressive clicks, drew out a slim folder. Inside there was a single fresh newspaper clipping, which he passed to Ruth and Osaya. Tobias had already seen it.

'This is a story' he explained, 'that appeared recently in the Telegraph. It concerns a man called "Angel" Donaldson. As you can see he is thought to be interesting to the British public for the reason that he knew Amin twenty years ago, when the two of them served together in the King's African Rifles, fighting against the Mau-Mau on the jungle slopes of Mount Kenya. Now Donaldson gives the impression that he considers Amin to be "a British product gone wrong," or something like that – a sergeant-major who should never have been made a dictator. You know the line. There are plenty of British army officers who have been prepared to give Hippo that sort of a reference. What's different about Donaldson is that he thinks the British are in some way responsible for Amin's misdeeds, and that they should help Uganda to get rid of him.'

'How can this man be of use to us?' Osaya looked up doubtfully from the clipping.

'Donaldson is quite an interesting fellow apart from his disapproval of Amin. In late 1967 he enlisted as a mercenary in Biafra and stayed there for most of the war. Not for the money, but because he's the adventurer type and also a bit of an idealist. According to this article, although he's settled down now, he still gets restless sometimes for what he calls "the good old days". A trained British officer with plenty of experience of unconventional warfare, a tough former mercenary who has known Amin intimately and more or less says that he thinks he should be bumped off . . . isn't this a man who might be able to help us?

'What I am suggesting is that we admit to ourselves that we have been labouring under too many illusions and disadvantages. If we want Operation Hippo to succeed we must have a professional, a man who knows how to kill, to do the job for us. I think Mr. Donaldson might be willing to take it on. What do you think?'

Michael took off his glasses and rubbed them on his sleeve, peering short-sightedly round the table at each of them in turn. Tobias, with whom he had already discussed the idea, at once nodded his approval. But Ruth seemed to hesitate. It was not because she didn't agree with Michael's proposal – it struck her as by far the most sensible suggestion any of them had come up with yet – but because somehow it revealed Michael to her in a new light. She had always known him and, indeed, once loved him for a gentle, studious and slightly ineffectual character. They were also qualities she had found at times utterly exasperating. Since he had come back from Uganda she had noticed changes in him. It was hardly surprising after what he had been through, but he seemed bitter and hardened and was sometimes given to moods of dark despair. However, now she recognised about him a quiet and dignified authority, which commanded the respect of all and impressed her deeply. She was suddenly full of admiration for him and it troubled her. In her confusion she stared down at her hands and twisted at a tortoiseshell bangle on her thin, elegant wrist.

'Ruth?' Michael's tone was hopeful.

She looked up quickly and said, 'If he'll do it, I think it's the right thing.'

Osaya was still reading the clipping, but shaking his head as he read. 'What makes anyone think this man Donaldson, "Old Etonian, former Guards Officer, now an estate agent living in Cheltenham," is going to leave his wife and children to risk his neck for us?' He looked round the table.

'You are all pretty crazy, you know. I think this idea is no good for us, Michael. Really I think we are better accepting responsibility for our own actions.'

'It's three against one – a democratic majority,' Tobias said rather smugly.

Michael carefully put his glasses back on. 'This decision must be unanimous.'

'Anyway, how would we pay the man?' asked Osaya. 'They say he's an idealist, but this is just a piece of paper. He will want money.'

There was a moment's silence, then Ruth said 'If we all decide to plump for him, and if he says yes and if he wants money, then I think I can get the money.'

'Osaya,' Michael put a hand on his arm, 'you are quite within your rights to hold a different opinion from the rest of us. But we must be all agreed on how to proceed. Think about it carefully and let us know your decision in the morning.'

Michael picked up the Donaldson clipping, put it back in the folder and slipped the folder into his briefcase. Then he snapped the Samsonite shut and rose to his feet, indicating in a business-like way that the meeting was over.

## TWO

The girl standing on the corner of the Old Brompton Road and Bina Gardens, waiting to cross the street, belonged to a type that is not uncommon in that part of London. Tall and slim with an attractive figure, she had a long oval face, pleasant enough and unmistakably English, but a little prim about the mouth and with a tilt to her nose that suggested a conviction of hereditary superiority. She was wearing a light-coloured raincoat, turned up at the collar, that looked insufficient proof against the blustery February afternoon. Her head was inclined forward so that the fringe of her dark chestnut hair, cut short and square like a pageboy's, obscured her eyes and added to the impression that she was in a hurry, if only to get home and out of the cold. As she turned into Drayton Gardens she stepped out at a brisk pace and the click of her heels along the pavement had the confident, no-nonsense ring which, as much as the expensive accessories she wore – the smart Gucci loafers and a battered but still elegant St. Laurent shoulder bag – identified her as a working girl from the upper strata of English society.

Watching her approach from the unlit drawing room window of her flat, Osaya Nagere, his square black thumbs hooked into the belt loops of his claret flares, did not see labels in the minor details of her appearance. Nor, if he had, would he have attached much importance to them. The girl in the mackintosh meant other things to him. As far as the way she looked went, he found her simply beautiful. Although it was not something he chose to broadcast, Osaya was an avid reader of comics and Sally Temple Owen reminded him a lot of Lois Lane, who was, of course, Clark Kent's girlfriend in *Superman*. After nearly two months of going out with her he still could not get over his good fortune, and as she stopped in the street below to look for her keys, he felt his desire for his comic-strip heroine mount within him.

Osaya moved back a little from the window so that she would not see him until she came into the room. The place smelt of paint and everywhere there were packing cases and tea-chests and furniture draped in dust covers. She had moved in a week ago and he was meant to be giving her a hand with the decorating, but it was a job that he felt to be somewhat beneath him. Previously she had lived in a tiny maisonette in Hampstead, which Osaya had found more to his liking than the vast, rambling apartment in this ugly red-brick mansion block. It struck him as old-fashioned and gloomy, though right now the dark, cheerless atmosphere of the room suited his mood. The morning's meeting with the friends had left him feeling resentful and more distressed than he knew.

He heard the key turn in the door of the flat. Even before it slammed shut she was calling his name, and then again as she moved through the hall, but he did not answer. She came into the room and in the semi-darkness he saw her reach out a hand for the light switch.

'Leave it,' he said softly. 'Don't turn on the light.'

'Osaya!' she yelled and dropped her bag. 'My God, you gave me a fright! What's wrong? Why are you standing there in the dark like that?' There was surprise, concern, but also a note of fear in her voice.

'Just leave the light and come over here.' He moved forward a little way to meet her as she came across the room to the window. There were no curtains and behind him the light from the street made a menacing silhouette of his stocky frame. She put her arms around him and hugged herself to his body, seeking reassurance.

Osaya stood quite still, letting the scent of her hair rise in his nostrils and the pressure of her cold, soft cheek against his increase of its own accord. She had unbuttoned her raincoat and he could feel the warmth of her body through her woollen skirt. She began to kiss him around the mouth, but deliberately he made no response.

'What's wrong, darling?' she whispered. 'Is something the matter? Have I done something to upset you? Tell me.'

Osaya felt an ungovernable frustration build up inside him and become confused with his fierce desire for this white girl, who was so civilised, so delicate and so rich. She had never been anything but good to him, but now he only wanted to hurt her. He did not answer. She smiled up at him and rubbed herself against his body. Her breathing quickened and she began to moan gently as he felt her tongue lay a trail of saliva that ran up from the corner of his mouth to his ear.

Suddenly Osaya stepped away from her. 'You white girls are all the same. You go out with us because you think we screw all day, all night and make you itchy for it and keep you satisfied. Am I your dog?'

He slapped her hard across the face. Sally's mouth fell open and she made a little sound, as if she wanted to speak, but nothing came. Then she burst into tears.

Osaya laughed and said thickly 'Now I'll show you what you really are, you bitch. This is what you want from me, so you can have it.' He came forward and, bending down swiftly in front of her, picked up the edge of her skirt and the long raincoat and lifted them clear over her head. Then, enveloping the top half of her body with her clothes, he pulled her down in one easy movement on to the bare parquet floor.

Sally screamed, her voice muffled by her skirts. She struggled to pull free, but Osaya held her easily with one hand, while the other reached up around her waist and found its way inside the elastic of her tights. He began to peel them from her, despite himself grunting with excitement as the pale skin of her thighs was suddenly revealed in the cruel light of the street lamps that came in through the bare windows of the apartment. She kicked and rolled and fought, but as his hand went between her legs and found the dark mound of pubic hair moist with desire, he laughed at her. She swore at him harshly, then urgently as he turned her over on to her front and pulled her up on to her knees. The girl's smooth, ivory bottom reared up invitingly before him. He let go of her for a moment to prepare himself, but Sally's resistance had gone. She made no effort to escape, and when he entered her from behind with a brutal thrust, she moved back hard against him.

It was after midnight when Osaya returned to the flat in Drayton Gardens. Sally, who had already gone to bed, was waiting up for him, but made a point of not asking him where he had been. Before either of them spoke they made love again, only this time without cruelty. They exchanged gentle caresses. Osaya apologised for what had happened earlier and she smiled and kissed him and forgave him. She also let him know with a movement of her body that she had been a willing victim. He felt a new stir of excitement at her brazenness, for in spite of what he had said to her that afternoon, the white girl's hunger for him was a source of pride as well as pleasure. But Osaya had other, more important things to think about and he pleaded tiredness.

Since the meeting with the friends, he had been turning over Michael's proposition in his mind. But he found it almost impossible to consider the case on its own merits. He could not separate the idea that they should hire a professional to do the job from the implication that he was not up to it himself. Clearly the others had lost confidence in his capability as military commander. 'Charles Bronson' was suffering from wounded pride and he knew it, but it made his decision no easier. And there was something else. The others were all Baganda and Acholi and he was a Lango. Perhaps they were trying to get rid of him. He knew Tobias did not like him – had he persuaded the others that as an outsider he could not be relied on? And what if they were right? How could he be the one to jeopardise the whole mission? But a mercenary . . .

His insomnia and restlessness caused by the anguish of indecision became too much for Sally and she broke her resolve.

'Why don't you tell me what's wrong?' she said simply and with affection. 'Perhaps I can help, you never know. Is it something to do with . . . the friends? Has something happened?'

Osaya thought carefully before he answered. Although sworn to secrecy along with the others, he had already told Sally something about Operation Hippo. He had done so because ever since their first meeting, when he discovered that she had spent most of her childhood in Uganda, and that her father, who had been in coffee there, had good reason to hold a personal grudge against Amin, he had felt sure that he could trust her. Since then nothing that she had said or done had made him want to change that opinion. Rather, her own hatred of Amin, her horror and sadness for what was happening in Uganda made him doubly sure of her reliability. He had even tried to persuade the others – strongly denying that he had told her anything – that she could become a useful member of the group. They had not wanted her, of course, but he felt sure there would come a time when they would recognise that her social position, her wealth and the simple fact that she was white might come in undeniably handy.

After due consideration he told her about the plan to hire Donaldson and, what was more difficult for him, revealed his doubts about his own competence and his resentment at being passed over.

Sally, sympathetic, soothed and flattered him. 'I think you're tough and brave and beautiful and I know you'd make the best killer in the world . . .' Her eyes were bright with admiration. Sometimes before he had noticed that talk of assassination excited her, but tonight it was different. 'I don't want to lose you. You've become precious to me, Osaya.'

'But I want to get him for myself, to revenge my father's death, to pay him back for these.' He pulled her hand on to the puckered scars that covered his kneecaps.

'My poor darling,' she murmured, 'but what about the others? They're not made for this sort of thing, you know that. They want revenge, too, but they'd only get themselves killed. And their inexperience would put you in danger. Why not let them find out more about this man – whatever his name is? If he agrees to do it and is successful, you would still have your revenge. The important thing for Uganda surely is that Amin should be removed, and will it really matter then whose finger it was that pulled the trigger?'

For a long while Osaya was silent. 'All right,' he said finally, 'I think you're right. I have been proud and foolish. I should tell them I agree. I'll say to Michael in the morning.'

She kissed him gratefully and they said goodnight and lay together in the darkness. But still Osaya could not sleep. When he did eventually doze off, his dreams that were not dreams at all but memories of a nightmarish reality took him back to a room in Makindye. His ears filled with the sickening sound of car axles smashing down on innocent skin and bone. Faces he had known turned to red unidentifiable mush before his eyes as the blood of his friends splashed over him. The corporal kept repeating, 'Leo iko kazi, leo iko kazi, leo kazi . . .'* Wielding a rhinoceros-hide whip, he forced them down on to their hands and knees to pick up the evidence of yesterday's work – teeth and eyes and broken bits of bone that littered the floor like debris after a party. They had to sluice the blood from the walls.

Now the corporal was torturing him again, making him kneel on a bed of nails with his head inside the steel rim of a lorry wheel. Another man sat on his head pressing his ear to the metal while the corporal beat the outer edge with an iron bar and the terrible noise reverberating through

* There is work to be done today.

his head seemed to reach beyond the limits of endurance.

Osaya woke abruptly, covered in sweat and trembling all over. He reached out for the girl but the space beside him was empty. Then he noticed that the light was on. Sally Temple Owen, in her flower-patterned Laura Ashley nightgown, was sitting up at a makeshift dressing table, reading a book.

## THREE

A large overweight black labrador, greying about the muzzle, stood and barked obstinately at the two Ugandans from the other side of the garden gate. Tobias, who had an unreasonable fear of dogs, backed away, leaving Michael clutching his Samsonite and fiddling with the latch. A strip of natural, raw timber-look wood gave the name of the neat neo-Georgian house as 'The Bundu,' which struck them both as very inappropriate. Tobias felt uncomfortably out of place in this Cheltenham suburb that reminded him strongly of fashionable Tank Hill in Kampala – a relic of colonial Africa and white man's rule.

'Whisky, down boy! Quiet, you idiot dog!' A small, boyish-looking man with wavy blond hair suddenly appeared from behind the house and came springing down the path towards them. He was wearing grey flannels, a track-suit top and plimsolls and carried a pair of gardening shears in one rubber-gloved hand.

'Hello there! Jambo and all the rest of it . . .' he smiled broadly at his visitors as he approached. 'I'm afraid I've forgotten most of my Swahili! Don't mind Whisky here, he's absolutely harmless. Barks like a fool but a damned good watchdog. Come in, come in. Alec Donaldson. How are you?'

He opened the gate and shook hands with Michael and Tobias, who introduced themselves as he herded them through, at the same time trying to restrain the labrador by its zebra-skin collar. Michael had a sinking feeling that Donaldson was not their man. A glance at Tobias told him that he felt the same way.

Five minutes later they were sitting awkwardly on the

edge of a comfortable Chesterfield sipping dry sherry and carrying on an embarrassed conversation about Africa. They might have been discussing different continents. During these preliminaries two tow-headed children trooped into the room and stared at the black men on the sofa. They were told to say hello and shake hands, but instead they ran away, dissolving into giggles outside the door.

'Silly and rude! Come back at once and apologise!' their father called after them. He frowned disapprovingly, then grinned at the Africans, who insisted politely that the children should not be brought back; and the man they had chosen to be their assassin acquiesced.

'We would very much like to discuss General Amin,' Michael began tentatively. 'I think I mentioned to you on the telephone . . .'

'Ah yes, friend Idi! The old rogue. Well, what do you want to know?'

Michael hesitated and looked at Tobias, but Donaldson didn't wait for their answer.

'You know, in those days he really was quite different, a first-class soldier. He was slim and fit, always well-turned out, not all gone to fat like he is now. And he was immensely strong. You know, he used to insist on carrying the Bren gun, along with his rifle and all the magazines, even when it wasn't his job. Looked like a bloody Christmas tree. He was thick as a post, of course, but very popular with the men and I know that for a fact because I was his platoon commander. They respected Sergeant Amin not just because of his size, but because he was damned brave. He literally knew no fear. I remember once he charged a Mau-Mau bivouac in the forest. Went in single-handed with the Bren . . . I can tell you it was a jolly impressive performance. I tried to get him a Military Medal for that, but the recommendation went astray. Then the bloody idiot went and caught the clap and that put him out of the running for his Long Service and Good Conduct . . .'

'Good conduct,' Tobias interrupted. 'Mr. Donaldson, you are talking about a man who is responsible for massacring and torturing thousands, perhaps hundreds of thousands, of innocent people – a mass murderer, a monster, and you can mention his good conduct.'

'Now don't get me wrong, old chap.' Donaldson pushed a hand through his tousled hair. 'I'm talking about what Amin was like twenty years ago. I thought that's what you wanted to know. One of you said something about doing research for an article . . .' He looked up at them; his china-blue eyes had a puzzled glaze.

"We are doing research for an assassination – ' Tobias bit off the sentence. It was not what he had meant to say.

'Well, I'll be blowed!' Donaldson gave a low whistle. A man of forty-five or more, his expressions and mannerisms were those of a twelve-year-old schoolboy.

Aware that they had made a mistake, Michael felt that there was nothing for it now but to go ahead and put their case. 'We read in your interview that you disapproved of Amin and that you believed he could only be removed by an assassin's bullet. You said it would take a man who knew him to do the job.'

'Yes, but hang about – you're not suggesting that . . .'

'We might as well speak plainly. We have come here to ask you, who have experience in such matters, to kill Amin and liberate Uganda from its pestilential dictator.'

'Angel' Donaldson whistled again, and springing from his chair strode over to the french windows, where he stood with hands thrust deep in his track suit pockets, staring silently out over his tiny rose garden, as if beyond it stretched away the endless savanna of the African bush.

'Dammit, you know,' he spoke softly without turning round, 'There's nothing I'd like better than to have a crack at old Idi . . .'

'Then you'll help us?' Tobias interrupted eagerly.

Donaldson turned from the window and began to pace up and down the room, taking enormous strides for so small a man. He stopped by the edge of the carpet and kicked at it thoughtfully with his plimsoll as if he was replacing a divot after a rather wild swing at golf.

"Now half a tick, this one needs serious consideration. I suppose you're thinking of the Commonwealth Conference in June. Do you really imagine he'll come?'

Michael and Tobias looked at each other, then Tobias said, 'We have a big hunch that he will. Once Amin would have thought twice about leaving Kampala for so long, but now there is little opposition left for him to fear. Unless *all* the Commonwealth countries can agree to ban him – and the African Nations will make that very difficult – the British Government will not dare to keep him out. We think he will come, and we are planning for that eventuality.'

'What exactly did you have in mind?' Donaldson gave them his quizzical blue-eyed stare.

'Amin has a genuine affection for the British Army.' Michael said. 'As you yourself pointed out he is a product of the barrack square, a corruption of the Sandhurst ideal. Unlike some British officers who served with Amin in the K.A.R. you have not kept in touch with him or been back to Uganda since the coup . . .'

'Right!' Donaldson nodded. 'So what are you driving at?'

'When he comes to London security will be very close, but he will certainly want to see some of his old friends. As his former platoon commander you will have a very good chance of getting an audience with him.'

'The O.C. approach doesn't work with Amin any more.' Donaldson spoke now with authority and a new seriousness. 'He probably wouldn't agree to see me, I'm an unknown quantity now. The man is totally unpredictable, of course, but he has a phenomenal nose. He'd think it suspicious that I'd never tried to get in touch before – for instance, when he was in London in '71.'

'You could write a letter, explaining that you were away at the time,' suggested Tobias.

'Any attempt that involves getting close to the man, I would say, is doomed to failure. He may be gross and clumsy and basically stupid, but if there is a hint of threat in the air, he'll get wind of it and then he's as cunning, as agile and twice as dangerous as a wild buffalo.'

'We could afford to pay you.' Michael sensed that Donaldson was preparing to back down.

'It wouldn't be the money I'd do it for, but just out of interest – how much can you raise?'

'One thousand pounds, two?' Michael said uncertainly.

'For a man to risk his neck on a job like this? You'll need five down, and five more for successful completion.'

'But will you do it?'

Donaldson hesitated. Before he could reply the door of

the sitting room swung open, revealing one of the children standing shyly, twisting his hands behind his back.

'Mummy says to tell you that lunch is ready and we're having roast beef and Jennifer's getting hungry."

'Thank you, William.' Donaldson looked embarrassed and cleared his throat. 'You can tell her I'm just coming. Run along now and help with the table.'

'It's already laid. And I'm hungry, too.'

'William!' Donaldson gave him a stern look and the boy ran off, banging the door and shrieking with laughter.

'I'm sorry about that. Little tyke, I should tan his hide. Well, gentlemen, I wish I could invite you to stay for lunch, but I think in the circumstances . . .'

Michael and Tobias had already risen to their feet and were making their apologies for staying too long.

On their way down the garden path with Donaldson walking ahead and the labrador trotting hopefully behind, Michael said politely, 'We haven't had your answer, Mr. Donaldson.'

He turned and walked backwards in front of them, breaking into a little jog to avoid tripping over the dog. The sun came out from behind a cloud. Donaldson screwed up his eyes and for a moment the lines of his face revealed his age. He stopped by the gate.

'I'm a married man with a wife and a couple of sprogs. That means responsibilities. But I approve of what you're trying to do, even if I still have a soft spot for the old bastard.

'Let me tell you something interesting. Before I resigned my commission with the K.A.R., it struck me that Amin was going to be wasted in the army. In those days, of course, there was no hope of promotion for your chaps beyond the rank of sergeant. I knew that he'd started out as an army cook and I thought quite seriously then of bringing him back to this country to be a sort of chauffeur-cum-gardener for my parents-in-law, who lived in Perthshire. I put it to Amin, but after due consideration he turned it down, though he said he liked the idea of living in Scotland. Just think if he'd said yes, how different the history of Uganda might have been . . . And, for that matter, the history of Scotland.'

Donaldson grinned but, seeing that the two Africans did not share his amusement, he quickly adopted a more earnest expression. 'I don't want you to think that I'm not taking your offer seriously. What's more, it appeals to me like the blazes. To tell you the truth I sometimes get a bit bored with all of this.' He made a quick sweeping gesture that included most of Cheltenham. 'But I need some time to think it over, to consider the practicalities as much as anything. Give me two days and I'll let you have my answer. Where do I get in touch with you?'

For a moment Michael hesitated, then brought out pen and notebook and quickly wrote down his address in North Kensington. He tore out the page and handed it to Donaldson.

'It's all right, you can trust me. If I decide against it, I'll dispose of this and forget that I ever met you. Whatever happens, good luck.'

With that 'Angel' Donaldson reached over the gate of 'The Bundu' and clasped each black hand in his with a firm, manly grip, then turned and jogged up the path towards the house with Whisky lolloping along at his plimsolled heels.

On St. Valentine's Day Michael Kinkasa received a letter postmarked Cheltenham. It was typed on headed notepaper with an embossed logo of a Georgian façade. Under the names of Metcalfe and Donaldson, Chartered Surveyors, the letter read as follows:

Dear Sir,

With reference to your recent enquiry regarding the aforementioned property, we regret to inform you that the owners have since decided to take it off the market.

We have pleasure, however, in enclosing details of further estates, which we trust may be of interest.

Yours sincerely,
Alec Donaldson, A.R.I.C.S.

Michael had been expecting Donaldson to turn down their offer, but he was irritated by the pointless subterfuge of the formal estate agent's letter. He imagined Donaldson dictating it to his secretary – which meant, of course, there would have to be a file copy. Idiotic of him, but typical, he thought, of that overgrown schoolboy. Then he noticed that the letter had not been signed; it was also poorly typed, which made him think that perhaps Donaldson had done it himself. Even so, it seemed a futile exercise.

The enclosures consisted of the usual agent's roneoed list with a series of four or five-line descriptions of a variety of accommodation in the Cheltenham area. Michael cast his eye rapidly over the document and then locked it away with Donaldson's letter in his Samsonite briefcase. Some of the grander, more expensive properties were described individually on stiff white paper like invitation cards under the Metcalfe and Donaldson motif. These he looked at more carefully for the simple reason that the cards were attractively produced. Among them he came across a joker.

It was a card advertising a car hire firm. Cheaply printed on a yellow background, it had a royal blue silhouette of a limousine with an aerial sending out zig-zag radio waves in all directions. The card was well worn and curled at the corners. He assumed it must have been put in with the others by mistake. Then he noticed that Beacon Radio Cars operated from London – not Cheltenham. Their motto was '24 hours Any Time – Any Place' and they offered A/c facilities for Passengers, Parcels and Contracts. The word 'Contracts' made Michael pause. He turned the card over. On the back was scrawled in an uneducated hand – he doubted it was Donaldson's – 'Ask for Gerry. We wore the red scarf.'

## FOUR

The car parked outside the house in Ashbourne Grove, a quiet residential street off Chiswick Lane, was a bright, rust-coloured 1974 Ford Granada. The man in the leather coat, of a less obtrusive shade of brown, supporting himself with one outstretched hand against the roof of the car, appeared to be somewhat the worse for drink. His coat was unbuttoned and the long folds hung forward obscuring his actions. Passers by, had there been any at that time of night, might have guessed that he was having difficulty in getting his key into the lock of the door. They would have been right, more or less.

He cursed softly to himself as he tried one key after another from the large gaoler's ring that hung from his wrist. Then he started back again on the section of Ford types. Usually it went much quicker than this. As he worked he listened rather than kept watch, but there was no movement in the street. At last the lock clicked back. The key ring disappeared inside the sleeve of his coat. Straightening up, he opened the door and, looking round once, eased himself into the driver's seat. Matching the ignition key took less time. He started the motor, switched on the side lights and, checking the gauge for petrol, released the handbrake and pulled away from the kerb. At the bottom of the street he turned right, then left out of Chiswick Lane into the fast-moving traffic of the Cromwell Road Extension and headed back into Central London.

In Knightsbridge he turned right across the Brompton Road and drove down behind the back of Harrods, taking his usual short cut to Belgravia via Hans Crescent, but instead of crossing Sloane Street he slowed to a crawl and began to cruise south along the dark and narrow length of Pavilion Road. When he saw the Jaguar parked on the corner near the junction with Pont Street, he turned off his lights and drove past as instructed. Then after fifty yards or so he pulled into an empty space outside a garage door and shut off the engine. Removing the key from the steering column he produced a lump of plasticine from his pocket and took an impression. He wrapped the plasticine in cellophane then put it back in his pocket, keeping the key in his hand while he sat and waited. He could hear the raucous sounds of a party in progress somewhere further down the street. After a few minutes he heard footsteps approaching. He wound down the window.

'So this is she?' He nodded, looking straight ahead of him. The palm of a glove came through the window. He handed over the key. A brown envelope was passed back. He checked the money: it was twenty pounds short. He considered asking for the difference, making a complaint, but lost his nerve. There were two of them and he needed a drink, not a beating. One opened the door and bending down, so that he just caught sight of a fat bearded mouth, said: 'It's not quite what we had in mind, but it'll have to do. Goodbye, Schulz.'

He struggled across the seat and got out by the passenger door. Following instructions, he walked away from the Ford and down the street without looking back. When he had gone fifty yards he stopped to light a cigarette, then he walked on.

He had left his own car parked outside the church on the corner of Beauchamp Place and Pont Street. They had told him not to bring it, but he'd been damned if he was going to walk from God knows where. The sight of the battered grey Mercedes gleaming in the aura of the church's floodlighting was somehow reassuring. He climbed in and sat there, motionless for a second or two, breathing deeply through his nostrils. Then he opened the dashboard and took out half-a-bottle of cheap cognac. He unscrewed it and swigged back several mouthfuls. It made him feel a little better.

Presently he drew off his thin leather gloves and carefully laid his hands at 'two o'clock' on the ersatz-ivory steering wheel. They were small delicate hands, surprisingly pale with slim, tapering fingers. They had been recently manicured and Schulz admired the work on his nails and cuticles, stretching out his elegant fingers to the full. Then suddenly he tensed and gripped the steering wheel as shame and anger at the humiliation he had suffered swept over him.

It was not just being cheated of the money, but the fact that he had come this low. And for a lousy hundred pounds. It had not been like this once. He remembered the green and red of the Legion – 'Honour and Fidelity.' That final attack against Onitsha by the Commandos of Ahoada Strike Force – a bloody wipeout, a terrible defeat, but by God it had been glorious. And now he was reduced to this . . . He was not a criminal. Schulz pulled the rear view mirror round and stared fiercely into his dull stone-coloured eyes. Then, all at once he sank back and relaxed into the comfortable leather of the Mercedes. He smiled wearily to himself. A man who spent most of his time alone, he often used physical expression to illustrate his inner dialogue. Leaning forward he switched on the two-way radio and picked up the mike. With his thumb over the red 'call' button, he spoke into it with only a trace of accent.

The same morning he received the letter from Donaldson, Tuesday, 14th February, Michael had communicated the news to the friends and called another meeting for the following evening to decide what was to be done. Over the telephone he had given no details about the letter or its enclosures, letting them know only that the arrangement had fallen through. In Tobias's case, since they were living together, he had shown him the letter and all the enclosures – except the card from Beacon Car Hire.

Michael felt that he had made a fool of himself over the Donaldson episode and he had no wish to repeat the mistake by suggesting to Tobias that it might be worth following up the curious message on the back of the card. Since he had every intention of doing just that and guessed that money would almost certainly come into it, he did not want Tobias, or any of the others, to veto the suggestion on the grounds of unnecessary expenditure. After paying the price of two return tickets to Cheltenham, they would not take kindly to his hiring limousines.

Michael waited until late that Tuesday evening before leaving the flat to telephone. Taking the yellow and blue card with him, he told Tobias he was going out for a walk, which was true enough since there was no 'phone in the house and the nearest kiosk that hadn't been vandalised was down on Ladbroke Grove.

Although he needed to be alone to make the call, the inconvenience irritated Michael, as did everything about their living arrangements. Since returning from Uganda they had been sharing two rooms at the top of a condemned house in Swinbrook Road, a derelict back street that runs to a dead end of corrugated iron hoardings under the shadow of Westway. They paid a small rent to a Ghanaian friend of Michael's from his London University days, who had moved to Birmingham on a teacher training course but wanted somebody to keep his 'London place' going. Living on Social Security, doing odd jobs at weekends for a furniture dealer in Ledbury Road, and with help from

Ruth, they just about managed to make ends meet.

Michael found life in North Kensington, which has a high density of West Indians, a people whose culture he neither understood nor felt in any way drawn towards, squalid in the extreme. Tobias could only compare it with Kampala and he did not find so much to complain about, but the two Africans remained aloof from what many regarded as a friendly and relaxed community. Both felt superior to the other blacks in the neighbourhood and resented being lumped together with them through poverty and by the inability of most white people to make a distinction which they considered should have been glaringly obvious. Michael made a point of never going out unless he was properly dressed in suit and tie, and even when he didn't need it, he usually took along his Samsonite briefcase as well.

In the awkward confines of the telephone booth he had difficulty in getting the briefcase open. He took out the card and dialled the first of the two numbers, letting it ring for some time. There was no reply. He tried the second number and almost immediately a voice answered, 'Beacon Car Hire.' Pushing in his 2p, Michael waited for the pips to finish, then erring on the side of formality, he enquired politely if he might speak to Gerald.

'Gerald? Hang on.' The voice became muffled. 'We haven't got a Gerald here, have we Frank?' Then it came back, 'Sorry can't help. Have you got the right number?'

Michael assured him that he had, then after an awkward pause he said, 'I am wearing a red scarf.'

'Are you really? It must look very nice on you. But this is a mini-cab firm, not a boutique.'

'Gerry told me to ring him at this number.'

'Gerry! Now I'm with you. You mean Schulzy, or Dieter the Meter, as we call him. He got a bit browned off with the Gerry handle. He's off tonight. You'll have to take another. So what can I do you for?'

'Actually I wanted Gerry. When will he be available, please?'

'Schulz is on again tomorrow morning at 11.00. Where's it to?'

Michael had prepared himself for this question. 'I want

to visit Kew Gardens.'

'Kew Gardens . . . And your address?'

'I can be waiting for him outside the Gaumont Cinema in Notting Hill Gate at, let us say, 11.30.'

'Fair enough. Do you have a 'phone number where we can contact you?'

'No, I'm sorry.'

'Name?'

Michael hesitated. 'Mr. Donaldson.'

On the morning after the job – if you could call it that – Schulz lay on his bed, smoking cigarettes and reading a magazine, putting off signing on for work until the last possible moment. It was a Wednesday, which meant going on at 1100 hours. It was now 10.35. He could afford another ten minutes in bed, time enough for one 'strip and remount,' then five minutes at the window.

Schulz's window looked out from a bedsitting room on the top floor of a large, pleasantly deteriorating house in Geary Road, Willesden. The Tudor-style frontage needed repainting, the garden fence leaned at an odd angle and some of the guttering had come adrift from the roof, but the garden was neatly kept and the whole character of the place was one of unfussy gentility. A thick growth of ivy had been allowed to take over the back of the house because the landlord liked the way it looked. Schulz had cut it back from around his window so as not to obstruct the view over Gladstone Park.

Under the surrounding eaves house martins nested in the summer and made a mess of the 'patio' below. Schulz had hung up lead-weighted strings outside to break their flying patterns – not because he was concerned about the landlord's patio (except for paying the rent he had no contact with the man), but because the noise they made and the sight of them hovering and dipping about at his window irritated him. He liked to keep the view absolutely clear.

Schulz lay on top of a stained, rumpled duvet propped up against equally unsavoury pillows. He was wearing maroon socks and a pair of light grey Terylene slacks, which he'd left unfastened at the waist, the fly-zipper half pulled up. Above the waist he was naked and the way he was lying, the white skin of his belly hung in thick folds over the opening in the top of his trousers. The creases between the folds glistened with little beads of perspiration, for the temperature in the room was well up into the eighties.

He stubbed out a half-smoked cigarette in an ash tray that lay beside him on the bed. It was already overflowing with butts and discarded chewing gum and brown apple cores. The addition spilled ash on to the duvet. Engrossed in his magazine, Schulz did not appear to notice. After a while he put down the magazine and looked at his watch. He swung his stockinged feet over the edge of the bed and sat up. He picked up the ash tray, carried it carefully across the room and emptied it into a wastepaper basket. Then he filled an electric kettle at the washbasin and plugged it into a socket beside a modern satinwood tallboy.

Waiting for the kettle to boil he opened the left-hand door of the closet and pushed it back on its hinges as far as it would go, so that the full-length mirror on the back of the door received maximum light from the window. He stood in front of the mirror, making a brief inspection of his appearance, then he said aloud, 'Captain Schulz, you have been accused of gross crimes against your own person. Negligence in personal attire brings disgrace upon the brigade. You have besmirched the name of the Fourth Commando.'

Hurriedly Schulz zipped up his trousers and stood to attention, pulling himself up to his full height – two inches short of six feet – and drawing back his strong muscular shoulders. 'Colonel Steiner, sir,' he said in a different voice, 'it will not happen again, I give you my word . . .' Then Schulz smiled and relaxed and, dropping the play-acting, moved closer to the mirror to study his reflection more carefully.

The remarkable thing about his face was that it gave an overall impression of ordinariness. And yet the individual features were in themselves quite striking. For instance, his hair was soft and silky and, for a thirty-eight-year-old man, a suspiciously uniform dark brown. He wore it short and shaved at the sides leaving an unusually large area of open skin behind each small and neat ear, which somehow gave his head an unprotected look. Apart from his nose which was coarsely made with wide fleshy nostrils, his features were as delicately formed as his hands. He had high, almost Slavic cheek bones, which gave his eyes – the colour of grey stone with whites more often than not slightly bloodshot – a barely noticeable slant, but a recognisable cruelty. His mouth and chin were those of a woman and had about them a beastly sensitivity. It was possible to see in Dieter Schulz, if one looked closely, something that made one shudder.

The kettle boiled and he made coffee. He carried the mug across to the window and set it down on the floor beside a chair carefully positioned for enjoyment of the view. He then went over to the door, checked that it was locked and came back to the bed. Quickly pulling aside the bed-surround, he knelt down on the floor where the rug had been and with the help of an ordinary kitchen knife jemmied up two floorboards. From the cavity he withdrew, one after another, three heavy sacks. Made of thick jungle-green canvas with leather facings, they bore some resemblance to golf club bags. Schulz laid each of the sacks on the bed, making deep impressions in the duvet, then unzipping the first he drew out a rifle with telescopic sights and carried it over to the window, where he propped it against the window ledge beside the chair and the mug of steaming coffee. Then he came back to the bed and out of the second canvas sack produced two submachine guns with folding steel stocks. After considering both for some time he rejected one in favour of the other and replaced it in the sack. He picked up a newspaper from the pile of reading matter on the bed and with the preferred weapon under his naked arm walked slowly over to the window and sat down in the chair. He laid the newspaper on the floor at his feet and after taking a quick sip of coffee set about field-stripping the gun.

The 9 mm Uzi, which he had picked up from the Israelis while under contract to the Anyana guerillas in the Southern Sudan, was one of his favourite weapons. The gun had once saved Rolf Steiner's life. It had never yet let him down and, as submachine guns went, its overall performance left little to be desired.

Drawing out the folding metal butt until it clicked into position, he gripped the stock in his left hand and with his right thumb pushed forward the catch in front of the rear sight housing. He then raised the cover and, removing it from the receiver, laid it on the newspaper at his feet. Disengaging the bolt he withdrew it from the receiver together with the recoil spring, giving the whole assembly a short pull forward that gave a sharp metallic sound, a noise which made Schulz smile with pleasure. In quick succession he removed the extractor, the barrel, the trigger group and pistol grip and laid them out on the newspaper with the other parts of the weapon until the Uzi was completely dismantled. Then he had another sip of coffee and looked at his watch. It was ten to eleven. Timing himself he reassembled the Uzi. It took him thirty seconds.

Schulz leant forward and picked up the rifle, a Weatherby ·460 Magnum sporting rifle, which he had paid £500 for three years ago to a dealer who was in a hurry to get it off his hands. Schulz considered that he had made a bargain. Resting one elbow on his knee, which he had crossed and raised a little by going up on to the ball of his left foot, he put the rifle to his shoulder and looking through the telescopic sight, drew a careful bead on a middle-aged woman walking her dog four hundred yards away in Gladstone Park. He held his breath and pulled the trigger.

Schulz sat at his window for the next five minutes, sighting targets in the park, following their movements, then squeezing off at a critical moment – as a figure was on the point of disappearing behind a tree, as a child was about to rejoin its mother, or two people's paths happened to cross. Each time the firing-pin slammed forward with a dull click on the empty chamber, Schulz laughed aloud. It was not, as anyone watching might have been forgiven for thinking, the laugh of someone deranged but that of a man who took a reasonable pleasure and pride in the one craft at which he excelled and for too long had had too few opportunities to practise.

# FIVE

At the bottom of Ladbroke Grove, waiting at the lights outside Notting Hill Police Station, it occurred to Schulz that he was not obliged to pick up this passenger. All he had to do was drive around for a while, then call the despatcher and say he had failed to locate him. It was the fact that they had asked for him personally – 'Gerry' as those bastards at the pound used to call him – that worried him. Perhaps something had gone wrong with the Granada last night. More than likely it was just another bloody contract to provide transport. Sometimes they asked him to be the driver, but he always turned it down: the extra money was no incentive to risk prison for the incompetence of others. At least if he got caught stealing a car, it would be his own fault. Then he remembered the humiliation of last night. He did not have to do it. He turned left out of Ladbroke Grove and swung the long grey Mercedes into Holland Park.

It was the name Donaldson that intrigued him. It could be coincidence: somebody new, or one of his old 'clients' using a different name – but there was also another possibility. There had been a Donaldson at Onitsha, who'd joined the brigade just before Steiner had been taken to Libreville. He'd been a good enough soldier, though too much the British officer. Schulz had tried to contact him once or twice over the last five years after he came back from Uganda, in the hope of getting some work that suited his talents better than driving a mini-cab. But Donaldson had refused to see him. He wondered if it was the same man. It could mean a job. In anticipation Schulz's delicate hands tightened on the steering wheel of the Mercedes till the knuckles showed white under their pale blue-veined skin.

He moved into the right-hand lane and executed a sweeping 'U' turn that brought him round in front of the Gaumont. He slowed to a crawl. No sign of anyone who resembled Donaldson. No 'client.' Not even a likely passenger. The tall negro clutching a briefcase and umbrella he dismissed as waiting for a bus. Schulz felt disappointment and irritation pricking at the back of his neck. He cursed himself for having indulged the luxury of expectation.

He pulled into the kerb, stopping short of the bus stop, and switched off the ignition. He looked at his watch. It was 11.34. In the rear-view mirror he saw the black looking over to the car. Schulz shrugged his shoulders. At least it was an African. He could tell them a mile away, not just by the respectable clothes, but the way they stood and walked and moved – like bloody ostriches. This one looked as if he might be a Kenyan, certainly from East Africa, the educated type, probably a student and short of money, with his little gold glasses and the crack down the middle of one lens. Schulz hoped the nigger had the price of the fare.

As he approached, Michael recognised the blue and yellow card of Beacon Car Hire in the back window of the Mercedes.

'Mr. Donaldson?' The driver leant over and opened the back door for him. 'You want to go to Kew?'

Michael nodded and got into the car. They moved out into the morning traffic. He sat very upright against the red leather upholstery, as if there was danger in allowing himself to become too comfortable. He didn't like what he'd seen of the driver's face and there was a faint smell inside the car of Johnson's baby powder. He opened the window.

'So you like the fresh air?' the driver said, 'Me too. I was always the outdoor type.' He laughed heartily. 'Actually I served in the Merchant Navy for a number of years.'

'Really!' Michael coughed politely. 'Was that the British Merchant Navy?'

'Naturally, Mr. Donaldson.' The driver caught his eye in the mirror and smiled. 'My parents were German, but they emigrated to South Africa before the War. I came over here as soon as I was old enough to escape from home. Later I took British citizenship. But you look around this country now and you wonder if you did not make a mistake. Socialism is gradually destroying Britain. It spreads like a malignant disease creeps through the body and corrupts everything . . . How come you asked for me, Mr. Donaldson?'

The question took Michael by surprise. He had been intending to get round to the subject in his own time. But they were at Shepherd's Bush already and he could hear the meter under the dashboard ticking steadily. Prevarication would only cost him money. He decided to be circumspect, but stay as near to the truth as possible. If there was something in it the man would make some sign.

'A friend of mine recommended Beacon to me and said to ask for Gerry.'

'Ha! That's what they used to call me, I'm afraid, when I first came to this country. My real name is Schulz, Dieter Schulz. Probably an old customer. What was his name, out of interest?"

Michael hesitated. 'Actually he shares the same name with me – Donaldson. A coincidence. Only he is Alec, I am John.'

'Alec Donaldson?' Schulz sounded surprised. 'That rings a bell. To tell you the truth, it's who I was expecting after the call from the despatcher. I didn't like to say so when you first got in, but I was a little disappointed. He's more than a client, you see: Alec and I are old friends. But I haven't seen him for an age now. How is the old son of a gun?'

'Doing fine . . .' Michael had picked up a note of interest in Schulz's voice, hidden behind the forced carelessness. He knew it was up to him to make the next move. He remembered the word 'Contracts' on the card. 'Alec said you used to do contract work for him sometimes.'

Schulz glanced round. Michael thought his face looked less unpleasant now, yet there was definitely something odd about him.

'We were in the same line of business once . . .' Schulz hesitated, 'But that was in the good old days.'

'When you . . . wore the red scarf?' Michael hazarded rather self-consciously.

Schulz pulled up and suddenly swerved into the side of the road, creating momentary chaos among the traffic. He swivelled in his seat and Michael saw one hand move swiftly from the steering wheel to the inside of his coat. His dull grey eyes were vigilant, but the voice quite calm.

'I know my Africans fairly well, Mr. Donaldson, but I

cannot quite place you. Were you with us at Onitsha?' He looked at him more closely. 'No, I don't remember this face. What is it you want?'

'I am a University lecturer from Uganda,' Michael said simply. He felt a little unnerved by the intensity of the driver's stare, but he understood at last the connection between Schulz and Donaldson: it was what he had been hoping for. 'I'm not sure how to put this, but I want to know if you are in the market . . . well, to be frank, I need the services of a mercenary.'

Schulz gave a shout of laughter. Sinking back into his seat he put both small hands back on to the wheel of the Mercedes. 'Forgive me, old chap. I thought for a moment you were somebody else, a visitor from the past. In my profession one has to be extra careful. They were magnificent times in Biafra, but there were many who did not feel that way – especially about us soldiers of fortune. Some have long memories . . ." Schulz paused. 'And I was in the Congo too, you know, and in the Sudan until '71, but that's my story. Now what's yours? Why should you need my services? You don't look like a man to hire me. When I picked you up earlier I doubted you had the price of the fare.'

'I represent a group of like-minded people, Mr. Schulz. We have money enough to pay you.'

'Of course!' Schulz gave a smile of recognition. 'Perhaps I should tell you now, for I am a man of honour, that I cannot set foot inside Uganda.'

'We are hoping that won't be necessary.' Michael leaned forward. 'If you are interested, we can go on now to our destination. It's as good a place as any to talk.'

Schulz started the engine and pulled out into Chiswick High Road. They were still heading in the direction of Kew, but the meter, Michael noticed, had been turned off.

They walked in Kew Gardens for nearly an hour, neither of them showing the slightest interest in their surroundings. Most of the period was taken up with Schulz's life story, which Michael insisted on hearing before they went on to discuss other things. He guessed that much of it was coloured by the mercenary's imagination; but, as he would discover later, there was also a great deal that Schulz left out.

The earlier part of his life, drawn in a few predictable anecdotes describing his boredom as a child in the middle-class suburbs of Johannesburg, his longing for adventure translated into the hum-drum reality of emigrating to Britain in the 1950s, doing his National Service in Kettering and then the series of half-tried jobs that in the end always disappointed, emerged as without clear shape or direction. It was not of particular interest either to Schulz or his solitary listener and he glossed over it quickly, passing on to what he considered the real beginning to his life – his enlistment and initiation as a mercenary in the Congo.

Schulz had arrived in time to take part in the third and last battle of Katanga. Joining this late in the war, he experienced all the worst aspects of the mercenary life. He saw disorder and inefficiency, poor leadership and worse administration; officers who disregarded orders and took their own decisions, the easy discouragement of the men at minor setbacks, the fury and panic and accusations of treachery that broke out in the face of defeat – he saw nothing but weakness, muddle and cowardice and, taking part in the ignominious retreat to Luashi, where there was a near-mutiny before Denard's invasion finally pulled back into Angola, failure. The rewards had turned out far from equal to the dangers involved; the discomforts and deprivations had been extreme; but in all of this Dieter Schulz had only recognised one thing. He had found at last his true vocation. As a soldier of fortune, a foreign volunteer, he could boast now, there would always be a job for him somewhere in the world.

It was during the Biafran conflict that by his own account Schulz won his spurs, though what he told Michael bore little relation to the facts. Schulz's Biafra and, indeed, the rest of his 'military' career was in reality dominated by the influence of one man, the mercenary leader Rolf Steiner – a name as well known in the ranks of 'Les affreux' as Bob Denard, Mike Hoare, Jean Schramme or 'Taffy' Williams. Only the way Schulz told it – and undoubtedly it was the way he saw it too, because he was not so much a liar or merchant of tall stories as a man whose perception of reality tended to coincide with his own psychological needs – the relationship between the two men might have been reversed.

It was not difficult to see what it was about Rolf Steiner that had impressed and attracted the younger man. Steiner was a German and looked like one; tall, blond and handsome, he was as tough as any man can get, hardened by the experience of seven wars. As a teenager Rolf Steiner had enjoyed the distinction of serving in the Wolf Cub brigade of the Hitler Youth during the final days of the Reich. Later, after joining the French Foreign Legion, he fought in Korea, Indo-China, the Middle East and Algeria. As a mercenary in Biafra, recently promoted from being an N.C.O. in the 1er R.E.P. to 'Colonel,' he formed the ill-fated Fourth Commando Brigade, organising it along the lines of the Legion. With 'Honour and Fidelity' as their motto, they wore the green beret and the red scarf – green and red, the colours of the Legionnaires. Steiner himself, however, had chosen as the emblem of the brigade the Nazi death's head, which he'd had inscribed in white on a black pennant that fluttered from the bonnet of his white Mercedes. Schulz, who had joined one of the brigade's battalions, the 'Ahoada Strike Force,' was filled with admiration that reached the pitch of hero worship for the dashing Colonel Steiner. Utterly seduced by the glamour of brutality, he had pledged a special loyalty to his countryman, and while slavishly modelling himself on Steiner, at the same time tried to compete with him in the only way he knew how – by carving himself an even worse reputation for acts of gross cruelty.

After the series of defeats inflicted on the Fourth Commando, which following the fall of Aba meant the end for Biafra, Steiner's brigade was decimated in a last desperate attempt to take Onitsha. It was there the Ahoada Strike Force, the 'Commandos of the Red Scarf,' distinguished themselves in savagery: much of it directed against their own side as the mercenaries, Schulz prominent among them, cut down Biafrans who refused to go forward in that hopeless assault.

In describing these scenes to Michael, Schulz painted a picture of defiant gallantry in the face of overwhelming odds, of a glorious regiment's last stand, of heroism that went undecorated but not forgotten. When Colonel Steiner was arrested (after breaking down under strain and publicly insulting Ojukwu) and carted off to Libreville in handcuffs, Schulz stayed on in Biafra with a handful of other mercenaries until their contracts ran out in early 1969. Afterwards he went on a long planter's drunk. Then, while making up his mind what to do next, he heard that Steiner, whom no-one had expected to escape the death penalty, had been released from prison and had turned up again in the Sudan where he was already fighting another war. Without waiting to be invited Schulz had joined him there in the last week of November, 1969.

When the two 'Biafran' mercenaries arrived on the scene, the war in the Sudan had already been in progress for nearly fifteen years. It was regarded by many less as a struggle for independence by the south than a conflict between the northern Arab Muslims and the southern Anyana Africans, who were predominantly Christian. For some time the Anyana guerillas had been receiving material support from the Israelis, who saw it as a way of striking up at the under-belly of the Arab world. Indeed, when Steiner and Schulz joined the Anyana, they were a little embarrassed to find themselves fighting what was clearly an Israeli-backed campaign. What would turn out to be more significant for the two men was that the Israelis had also made themselves influential in Uganda in order to secure a base of sorts for their operations in the Sudan.

Unknown to the mercenaries, however, by the end of 1969 relations between Jerusalem and Kampala were deteriorating and by the middle of the new year they had become severely strained. The reason for this was that President Obote of Uganda had decided to move closer to the new military leader in Khartoum, General Nimeri, whom he regarded as a progressive, likely to settle the dispute which had for so long ravaged his country. In a bid to strengthen these links with Khartoum by 1970 Obote was preventing Israeli planes flying arms to the guerillas in the southern Sudan from refuelling in Uganda. What Obote did not know – and what was soon to prove so confusing to the mercenaries – was that the Ugandan army was still deeply involved with the Anyana guerillas in the southern Sudan. The commander of the Ugandan army at that time was none other than General Amin.

In August, 1970, Steiner and Schulz came out of the Sudan on a routine trip to make contact with a Ugandan army unit. Soon after they had crossed the border they were somewhat surprised to find themselves arrested by the Ugandan police and taken down to Kampala, where they were promptly thrown into gaol. What happened next was to play a significant part in changing the course of African history.

At the time of their arrest Steiner's diary had been found on him and confiscated, to be used as evidence against him. More important, the diary contained several references to General Amin's visits to the Sudan, as often as not accompanied by Israeli officers. Not only did it reveal the full extent of his involvement with the Anyana guerillas, there was also evidence that Amin had been recruiting large numbers of Anyana guerillas into the Ugandan army – for what purpose would soon become all too apparent. When Steiner was deported to the Sudan on Obote's instructions in early January, 1971, to stand trial in Khartoum, it became certain that the evidence contained in the diaries was to be made public. Amin was left with no choice. On 25th January, 1971, while Obote was attending the Commonwealth Conference in Singapore, the General made his move.

Michael stared at Schulz, not so much in disbelief – for he had already heard the same story from a different and more reliable source – as in wonderment. It was surely a trick of fate that the man he was planning to hire to get rid of Amin, had helped, however unwittingly, to bring him to power. As if he had read his thoughts, the mercenary smiled and turned away with a slight shrug of his shoulders.

They were standing under the palm trees in the main hall of the great greenhouse. It had been Schulz's suggestion to come in out of the cold, as if the muggy tropical atmosphere of the conservatory would provide a more suitable setting for his story. Michael noticed that little beads of sweat had formed on the open patches of pale skin behind the man's delicately moulded ears. He felt sudden revulsion and thought how right he had been not to bring Tobias to this meeting. If they came to any sort of arrangement, Schulz would need very careful explaining to the others.

'What happened to you when Steiner was taken to Khartoum? Were you deported too?'

Schultz began to walk, his hands thrust deep into the pockets of his leather coat. Michael followed.

'No, I was lucky.' He looked back with a grin. 'You know Rolf is still out there. He was found guilty and condemned to death, only Nimeri commuted the sentence. He is doing twenty years. Rather him than me in a Khartoum gaol.'

'What did happen to you?'

'Actually, I was not considered important enough to bother about.' Schulz laughed modestly, but it was not a convincing sound. 'I was kept in prison in Kampala until after the coup and then let free at the same time Amin released a few Baganda political prisoners. So I wasn't intending to stick around. I came home. To this . . .' He raised his car keys from his pocket and jangled them. The sound covered any sign he might have been giving away that he was not telling the truth.

After being released from Makindye prison Schulz had remained in Uganda for eleven months. He had been contracted by Amin to train special commando units for patrol work on the Tanzanian border. The job turned out to be rather different to what he had expected. Schulz soon discovered that he had been conscripted more or less to carry out Amin's purges of the Acholi and Lango tribes in the army.

Frightened by the scale and haphazardness of the killing and finally disgusted by what he was being forced to do, Schulz had protested to Amin himself in a brave moment that it was not proper work for a soldier. Amin had responded by promising to make him a General and give him a house with a swimming pool on Tank Hill, wives, a chauffeur-driven car, anything he wanted . . . For half a day Schulz had believed that this was to be his future. Then he had listened to the advice of a friend, who warned him that he was being set up.

By luck he had managed to get out of Uganda that same

night, but although he escaped with his life, Schulz did not come away totally unscathed. He was still haunted by the visions and noises of Mutukula and he knew that he always would be. The memory of the things that he had done there could not be erased.

# SIX

'She's in there getting changed and taking an absolute age . . . My God, you're not the African boy are you?' For a moment Maurice looked alarmed, but seemed reassured by Michael's unaggressive appearance. 'There's no-one with her, it's all right. Only do ask her to get her knickers on and out here to do some work. Friday's shots were un total désastre.'

He'd finally tracked Ruth down at the riverside studio where she'd been working last week and had gone round there that same afternoon after the meeting with Schulz. The photographer had not looked at all pleased to see him when he'd appeared at the door unannounced. At first he thought this was yet another of Ruth's affairs, but had soon recognised his mistake.

He pushed open the door to the changing room. Ruth was standing by the window staring out over the river. She held a red leather belt in her hands and was fiddling with the buckle in an absent way. Half undressed, she was still wearing her knee-length black leather boots (which she told everyone were from Charles Jourdain) although above them she had stripped to her underwear. In the light from the window the pale blue strips of silk against the warm brown of her skin looked, Michael thought, like patches of sky reflected in the muddy waters of the Nile. It was impossible for him to ignore her beauty. She was wearing no make-up and in the soft lashes of her large, calm eyes and in the tilt of her short upper lip, for once clean of lipstick, Michael recognised the girl he had loved before she had become caught up in another world. Her hair was tied in tight corn-row plaits which gave her the sweet innocent appeal of a young girl and accentuated the long graceful curve of her neck. Michael had never seen a black swan, but he imagined that they must look something like Ruth.

She greeted him demurely and reached for a towel, but made only the vaguest attempt to cover her body. Suddenly Michael longed to take her in his arms. He moved towards her, but at that moment she caught his eye and he lost his nerve.

'I had to see you before tonight' he said in a low voice. 'We're going to need the money after all.'

'What's happened?' Ruth's eyes widened. 'Has he changed his mind?'

'Not really . . . Look, I can't explain now.' Michael turned to check that the door was properly shut. 'It's a matter of ten thousand pounds and we must have two of those by the end of the week.'

'I've got it already.' Ruth smiled and added calmly, 'Do you want me to bring some tonight?'

Michael stared at her. 'You . . . I don't understand. You mean you have that much money in your own account?'

'Not quite, darling. But I knew we'd need it in the end, so I've been doing a little borrowing . . . it's better you don't ask me any more, you'll only get upset.'

'What you do with your private life is your own affair,' he said coldly. 'But where the friends are concerned you must not hide things. It could be dangerous. I must know where you got the money.'

'Three of the men who take me out, darling, are rich – only disgustingly rich.' Ruth was trying to sound sophisticated and light-hearted, but Michael detected a brittle quality in her voice. 'I told them the old hard luck story about my brother being in prison in Uganda and how the only hope of getting him out alive was to bribe the judges. It was very convincing and they were only too pleased to help. It's as simple as that, really. I told them if they talked about it and word got back to Uganda, my brother would be killed. There's no risk involved there.'

She gave a short laugh and turned away to the window, but Michael had seen the tears in her eyes and felt ashamed. Ruth's brother was already dead and so, as far as anyone knew, were the rest of her family. They had all disappeared in the summer of 1975 shortly after Paul had been publicly executed.

Ruth had only been back to Uganda once since she came to Britain in the late Sixties, but she and her brother had been particularly close. Some time later she discovered what had happened. A foreign journalist, arrested in Kampala on the grounds that he was acting suspiciously, had been found with a list of 'contacts' on him. All of them were subsequently arrested and killed for alleged involvement in a plot against the State. Paul Utegi's name had been on that list.

'I'm sorry, Ruth.' Michael turned to go. He wanted to say more, but there was nothing. 'I'll see you tonight . . . I think it's going to be all right.'

The room was dark, lit only by the faint glow from the window. Schulz sat in his chair gazing out over Gladstone Park. Behind him on the bed the three heavy canvas sacks lay across the duvet, unopened. Somewhere in the room a transistor radio tuned to Radio Three was playing a lively overture by Offenbach. Schulz kept time to the music by tapping his foot against the radiator.

He had thought everything over very carefully and decided that whatever happened he was bound to come out of it nicely. Providing the Ugandans' credit was good, by the end of the week he'd be two grand better off. And that was just the deposit. He was to get another thousand on the first of each month until June; then, if everything went to plan, he'd get the same again in one lump sum. Ten thousand pounds was not to be sniffed at; nor for that matter was five . . . and it was the five, the first five, that really interested him.

He'd considered getting in touch with 'Angel' Donaldson to check the Ugandan's story about giving him his name, but then he thought better of it. He would find out what the set-up was soon enough. No point in involving too many people. As it was, the idea of a group did not appeal to him, but if they were all like the one he'd already met he'd be able to handle them. The job itself presented a few problems, of course, but he'd enjoy getting round them – selecting the right weapon, finding the best angle, the vulnerable moment, the safe approach. On paper at least he should have fun planning the operation.

'Operation Hippo.' He gave a short laugh. It was too much like the movies, but then they were amateurs, and wog-amateurs at that. It was to be expected. The irony was that he knew their target better than any of them . . . only that was not something he could reveal. He had no particular feelings about Amin, one way or the other, and it was better so. What went on in Uganda had ceased to be his concern the moment he got out of the place. If he had bad dreams sometimes, it had nothing to do with this. Nor had vengeance. Remove Amin and some other Nubian goon would take over. But that was their problem.

Schulz pulled on his cigarette until it glowed in the dark. He consulted his watch. The red crystal numerals flashed 8.31. He had half an hour to get something to eat. And then it would do no harm to be a little late . . . no, on the contrary, at this stage in the proceedings it was better to show keenness. After all, until he got the first payment he was on approval.

He stood up and walked over to the bedside table picking his way carefully in his stockinged feet. He switched on the light and, dropping his cigarette into a half-drunk cup of coffee, began putting his weapons away. It was a pity really. He would have enjoyed taking it through to that moment . . . Imagine those ridiculous rows of medals coming up to focus in the scope sight of the Weatherby . . . a moment that would have made him famous in history. He would have had to come forward and give himself up, declare himself before the world press – the popular assassin – Dieter Schulz, assassin by popular demand. Otherwise, who would know? *Wie schade!* The chance of a lifetime to demonstrate his skill. It *was* a pity, but even if the British Government or the Commonwealth did not try to stop him, under no circumstances could he see Amin leaving Kampala and coming to London in June. All that really mattered was that the final decision was put off until the last moment. Then he would not only collect the two thousand, but the monthly payments also.

Schulz stowed the last of the canvas sacks, re-aligned the floorboards and pulled the carpet back into place. Then he applied a fresh sprinkling of talcum powder to his hands and slipped on his desert boots. Picking up his coat, after a moment's indecision, he walked over to the commode and opened one of the doors. There, briefly, he consulted his reflection and smiled at what he saw.

The meeting was not a success. Michael had expected difficulties, but realised later that it might have been better to wait a day or two before introducing Schulz to the friends. He had presented him as too much of a *fait accompli.* Tobias, who was upset at not being taken into his confidence until the last minute, accused him of breaking with the democratic tradition of the group. Ruth agreed that Michael had acted in a rather high-handed manner, but admitted that in the circumstances he might have been justified. Osaya, characteristically, wanted proof that the mercenary actually had a gun and knew how to use it. They had argued fiercely.

Michael had defended Schulz, telling them something about his history in the Congo and Biafra, but taking care not to mention (as they had privately agreed) his role with Steiner and the Anyana in the Sudan affair. As a marksman, he pleaded, there were few men in Europe who could shoot straighter than Schulz. If necessary they could check his record with the Epping Forest Rifle Club . . Schulz had given him that piece of information, but he had also checked with 'Angel' Donaldson. Using his own estate agent's code, he had asked him over the telephone whether the new property was sound. Although the conversation had quickly disintegrated into Havana-style farce, one fact had emerged from it quite clearly: Schulz, when confronted with a barn door, could always be relied upon to hit it.

His big mistake, Michael decided, had been inviting the mercenary to join them at the pub. He had appeared as an intruder in their circle. No-one had taken to him, and it was not really surprising: there *was* something unpleasant about the man. Osaya had very nearly walked out when he first sat down with them. Even later on, when they had driven around in the Mercedes and Schulz had put forward some interesting ideas for how they should go about the operation, which had impressed Michael by the show of expertise and the amount of thought he had already put into the project, the others had remained sceptical and, on the surface at least, unimpressed. In the end they had parted company on the understanding that the decision would be delayed until the day after tomorrow, when everyone would have had more time to think it over.

On their way home from the meeting, as he and Tobias were coming up under the railway bridge by Ladbroke Grove tube station, Michael began to suspect that they were being followed. Just to make sure, instead of taking their usual route they quickly crossed the road and turned left into St. Charles Square. While Tobias went on ahead, Michael hid behind the churchyard wall. Soon enough he heard footsteps hurrying past. Standing up he caught a glimpse through the cemetery gates of a tall man in a blue denim suit. Dark, bushy-haired with a hawk-like profile and sallow skin, he might have hailed from North Africa or the Middle East or, for that matter, Bayswater. Michael was only certain that he'd never seen him before.

He waited. Presently Tobias came doubling back and vaulted over the wall into the churchyard. They sat shivering together on a gravestone waiting for the coast to clear. Tobias complained bitterly that this was all Michael's fault for getting involved with a man like Schulz.

## SEVEN

Two days after the friends' meeting, on Friday, 17th February, news reached London of the death of Dr. Janani Luwum, the Archbishop and Head of the Anglican Church in Uganda. It was claimed that he had been killed in a car accident between the Nile Hotel and the headquarters of the State Research Bureau in the middle of Kampala. There was little evidence to support the claim. 'No-one in Uganda,' as one of his bishops later pointed out, 'not even a child at school, could believe that. We all knew, without a shadow of a doubt, that the Archbishop had been shot.'

Outside Uganda credibility had been equally strained. Throughout the international community the accident was denounced as murder. Worldwide reaction to the slaying of Archbishop Luwum and the two senior Ugandan cabinet ministers, who allegedly had been in the car with him, was unanimous in condemning the horrifying excesses of Amin's military régime. President Carter and other world leaders expressed their disgust at what had happened and the U.N. Secretary General, Kurt Waldheim, at once demanded an impartial investigation into the Archbishop's death. In Nairobi the All-African Conference of Churches called an emergency meeting to discuss the threat to Christians living in Uganda.

Press coverage of the story was extensive and it was widely held that, although he was enjoying the limelight, President Amin had been unprepared for the storm of indignation and protest he had aroused. His reaction to the accusations that he was responsible for the death of the Archbishop was predictably direct. At a Press Conference in Kampala a week later he opened with the words: 'I have heard that I was the one who shot the Archbishop. But it is completely untrue to say that. I did not shoot him. Those reports are false.'

Resplendent in his light blue air force uniform, he gave a relaxed performance that was a characteristic display combining aggressive defiance of the 'Zionist Imperialists' with expressions of 'his sadness' at losing his friend, the Archbishop. True to form the show ended by deflecting attention from the Archbishop's death to a wild story of an invasion plot, organised by 'sixteen smugglers' who had already been arrested and had admitted that with the help of 'foreign paratroopers from the United States, Britain or Israel' they were going to create confusion by killing prominent people in Uganda. In other words President Amin had uncovered another plot against himself.

In London the Archbishop of Canterbury, Dr. Donald Coggan, made it plain that he believed there was now justification to hope for the disposal of Amin by any means, even an assassin's bullet. 'I want to see his régime broken,' he declared – a sentiment that was widely shared by both Christians and non-Christians around the world.

Among the 'friends' Dr. Coggan's statement was taken as a formal blessing of their enterprise. All of them had gone separately to their respective churches to pray for the soul of Dr. Luwum, for any remaining friends and family they had in Uganda and for all Christians there. But they prayed hardest for the success of their mission.

The murder of the Archbishop, by bringing Amin's crimes and the plight of their country to the attention of the world, had strengthened their determination to go through with Operation Hippo. As a result, argument and indecision over the hiring of Dieter Schulz was quickly resolved. Tobias's fears that the mercenary was somehow responsible for their being followed that night in Ladbroke Grove were dismissed as groundless. It was well known among the Ugandans that the police, and particularly Special Branch, were keeping an eye on the nine hundred Ugandan exiles in London. It was assumed that their 'tail,' as Osaya knowingly referred to him, was probably a part of routine observation. They agreed unanimously that Schulz should make the attempt and that they would provide him with whatever assistance he needed.

There was one aspect of the Archbishop's death which did not bode well for Operation Hippo. Both Michael and Schulz saw clearly that the recent publicity over conditions in Uganda would increase the chances of Amin being banned from attending the Commonwealth Conference in June. But for different reasons they did not discuss the matter with their colleagues. On the following Monday Dieter Schulz duly received two thousand pounds as the first instalment of his fee for the elimination of Idi Amin.

## EIGHT

The green telephone rang. It was seldom that it rang and it had become obscured by the framed photograph of his wife and children. He had momentarily forgotten it existed. In all there were five telephones on his desk. He picked up one and then another. By the time he remembered about 'the green job,' as he called it, and reached an exasperated hand behind Maude, Jimmy and Phyllis, who were smiling at him from the balcony of the Park Hotel, Korçula – rather too aggressively for this difficult Monday morning – the ringing stopped. A moment later it began again. This time he snatched it up at once.

'Yes?' he roared against a whirr of pips.

The voice came through. 'Plover here.'

'Why did you ring off like that, Plover? It's frustrating.'

'I dropped my 2p . . ."

'Anything happening out there?'

'Not much, except they seem to think we're on to them.'

'You've been rumbled?'

'No. The man who has been following them. They think he's one of ours. Is he?'

'I sincerely hope not – I'll ask around.'

'I'd appreciate that. It could be very awkward.'

'Goodbye, Plover.'

Commander Bill Moffet replaced the green receiver on its cradle and moved the photograph of his 'loved ones' back in front of the 'phone. He sat back in his chair and yawned, then he leant forward slowly and examined his breakfast of two Rich Tea biscuits and a mug of black coffee as if there was something suspicious about it. There was. The mug was new. Decorated with a picture of the Queen and the inscription 'Royal Jubilee 1952–1977,' it was, he supposed, somebody's idea of a joke. He went back to reading the batch of clippings on the Archbishop's death. Suddenly he let out a guffaw of laughter.

The door of the office opened immediately. "Sir?"

Moffet looked up guiltily. 'Ask Inspector Loveridge to step in for a moment, would you, Sergeant?'

Bill Moffet had a light, precise voice that sounded out of place in such a large, untidy-looking man. He had a great grey head and a tired flabby face with big ears and a small pink mouth. His eyes were small and round and bright and what they saw they never forgot. It was inevitable that in the Squad Room they should refer to him as Elephant Bill. He knew about it and minded.

He took a sip of coffee and stared out of the window at the bare and dismal trees in St. James's Park, still smiling despite himself at Amin's statement about coming to

London in June – 'eager to give the British Government advice on the current chaotic economic situation in Great Britain.' It was difficult sometimes not to be amused by the lunatic aptness of his remarks. But if one began laughing at the man, there was a danger of forgetting his less funny side.

'Good morning, Bill. You wanted to see me?'

'That's putting it a little strongly. I am obliged to see you, Arthur. And to you it's 'Commander' this morning.'

'Ah! One of those.' Inspector Loveridge looked knowing and, stepping quietly into the room, slipped into the cheap orange fibre chair in front of Moffet's desk. Loveridge looked, as no-one on the force ever tired of telling him, exactly like everyone's idea of a policeman. His clothes were labelled 'plain' and his small old-fashioned face under a diminishing ring of Vaselined hair wore a pinched look around the eyes and mouth, which gave the game away at once. It didn't worry him for the simple reason that his appearance, which in spite of the jokes he found somehow reassuring, had not yet affected the way he did his job; and that for him was all that mattered.

The two men looked at each other across the desk. The tacit superiority of Special Branch over the C.I.D. was reinforced not only by his seniority but by the enormous size of Bill Moffet. Although they were friends he always made Loveridge feel uncomfortable. The 'Conference Squad' was also primarily a Special Branch operation and Arthur Loveridge, who had been seconded to it from Criminal Intelligence to take care of any ordinary detective work that might be necessary in setting up the security arrangements, did not consider himself in a very fortunate position.

'One of your C.I.D. lot appears to be trying out his hand at surveillance. That is *our* responsibility and I want him out of there.' Moffet looked solid.

"Sorry sir, I don't know what you're referring to."

'Come off it, Loveridge. Ugandan affairs . . .' he gave a short laugh. 'No, well I don't suppose you read that sort of thing.'

'I'm leaving all "that sort of thing" to you, sir. There's no question of C.I.D. surveillance."

'Plover says they're being followed. If it's not us, it's them. You'd better get on to it. Is there anything in the rule book which says the C.I.D. can't dirty their hands with counter-surveillance?'

'Plenty.'

'I want Plover left out of it.'

'So why so pissed off, Bill?' Loveridge was trying to diffuse the atmosphere, but the colloquial turn of phrase fell very flat.

Moffet began thinking aloud. 'I suppose it could be anybody – Russians, Cubans, Palestinians, Israelis, Libyans – even the C.I.A. Most likely the K.G.B. are behind it. They may be trying to use Amin's visit to cause trouble. My feeling is that pretty soon someone will start cleaning up opposition to him over here. I want to know who they are first and if there's a connection with Schulz, then I want them removed from the scene.'

'Right,' said Loveridge. 'And you want the others left alone?'

'But strictly.'

Loveridge lowered his voice. 'If he actually comes are we going to let them go through with it?'

'It's a possibility. Another would be to send you out to Kampala to do the job for them. That would save everyone a lot of embarrassment.' Moffet guffawed. 'Don't worry, Arthur, the Home Office are working on other ways to stop him coming. This morning I have to get off a report to F4 explaining why we can't guarantee the fat man's security.'

'But then what's the point of . . .'

'Arthur, I hope you aren't going to say something silly.'

'Plover could be wasted . . .'

'Do you mean that in the American sense? Remember, these are my people.'

'All right, Bill, and as far as I'm concerned, you can keep them.' Inspector Loveridge rose to his feet. He'd had enough for one morning and he had work to do. 'Why "Plover" anyway? It's a ridiculous name.'

'Herodotus first spotted the Egyptian plover, then Pliny wrote about the brave little bird that cleans the gums of crocodiles by darting into their jaws and feeding off the food that sticks to their teeth. It has a respectable literary pedigree, but what interested me more, it also has a trick of sitting on the backs of hippos and feeding from their ears.'

'Hence "Plover"?'

'You got it in one, Loveridge.'

# *Part Three*

# WHEN THE LION ROARS

## ONE

*Kampala, 6th April, 1977*
At four minutes to five Lieutenant Abdala, carrying a large Sony portable radio, knocked on the door of the President's office. He entered without waiting for permission, saluted smartly and approached the enormous chair in front of the window, placed the wireless on the low table beside it. Then he saluted again and withdrew.

The office was simply, even sparsely furnished. There was a large desk with seven telephones, a standard lamp and a side table with a silver tray containing a bottle of Drambuie and two beer glasses. Around the walls hung dozens of framed photographs of the President, many in the company of world leaders. One captured a tuxedoed embrace with Edward Heath. Another showed him in military dress, decorated to the nines, talking to Earl Mountbatten. In another, beside General Bokasa, President of the Central African Republic, who was loaded down with decorations, he stood proudly without a medal on his chest, but carrying a Field Marshal's baton under his arm. Above the desk hung three photographs – one of the Queen, one of Colonel Gadafi of Libya and another of President Amin wearing a glengarry, kilt and a very small white plastic sporran. On the floor beside the desk lay a Russian carbine and an RBG7 anti-tank missile launcher.

The chair in front of the window was the only piece of furniture in the room of African origin. It was the throne of a tribal chief, made of dark mahogany, decorated with carvings of Ugandan emblems and standing at least seven feet high. The seat was covered in white fur and the arm-rests were made of polished buffalo horns that curved upwards into dangerous looking points. Along one horn lay a large black hand.

At less than a minute to five the hand reached out and turned on the Sony. Immediately the office was filled with the sound of loud blaring music. The hand fiddled with the dial and the noise came down to a bearable level and a more or less recognisable tune. The hand kept time with the music, slapping idly against the buffalo horn arm-rest.

"That was the massed bands of the Malire Mechanised Battalion giving you a recital of 'The Teddy Bears' Picnic.' This is Kampala Home Service, U.B.C. calling. Now follows the five o'clock news.

'A military spokesman is alerting all Ugandans to be on the lookout for any approaching invaders or suspicious aircraft into Uganda. All must be vigilant for twenty-four hours, and once the invaders are spotted they should be reported immediately, be it during the night or daytime, to the nearest of the numerous military installations scattered in the country.

'This advice is directed to all civilians as well as towards the Armed Forces. Nobody should accept to be taken by surprise, hence he needs to report immediately. The military spokesman, however, says that this should not lead to any panicking. Ugandans should rather be on the lookout and act immediately.'

There was a long pause, then the voice continued:

'The Defence Council suggested today and unanimously recommended that H.E. the President, Al-Haji F.M. Dr. Idi Amin Dada, V.C., D.S.O., M.C., remain Life President for the following reasons.

'1. For having dedicated his life to work for the nation.

'2. He has done more for Uganda since Independence than any other ruler.

'3. The job he has done in a few years is comparable to a job done in a hundred years.

'In addition the Defence Council recommended that, with immediate effect, H.E.'s security arrangements must be reviewed and the security escorts strengthened. The nasty attack on his person at a very colourful ceremony of the new police passing-out parade in Kampala last June has not been forgotten.

'The Defence Council also expressed that sooner or later all Government Ministers might have to be military men, as civilian ministers appear to be playing a double game. Any minister, or anyone else for that matter, found not performing his duties with reasonable efficiency will have to relinquish his post immediately. Repeated warnings would merely amount to flogging a dead horse.'

Another pause. The hand began slapping impatiently on the buffalo horn.

"At an opening of a seven-day seminar designed to educate Government Administrators, Life-President Amin said today that Ugandans are already heroes because they have done the impossible: that is running their own economy. He said that the main street in Kampala from Jinja Road to Bombo Road is manned by Ugandans only, whether they are stupid or not. Marshal Amin stressed that he is respected by all leaders. No country, however powerful, has any say in Ugandan affairs.

'H.E. also warned chiefs never to allow religious leaders in their areas to mix religion with politics, because this would create a serious situation like that prevailing in Northern Ireland . . .

'Dr. Amin observed that exiles in Kenya and Britain are double talkers, who transmit false and malicious information to the B.B.C. with the aim of spoiling the cordial relationship now existing between Uganda and the U.K. President Amin has directed the Ministry of Internal Affairs to check on people travelling to Kenya by road without sound reason. Dr. Amin said that he has advised soldiers from various battalions to watch out for and take drastic steps on such characters, who transmit false rumours and baseless reports about Uganda.

'The grandfather of Uganda said that when the lion roars all the animals and the people in the area turn their ears to the source of the sound, but the lion is always a peaceful animal unless it is attacked, threatened or inconvenienced.'

The hand reached out and turned off the radio. For several minutes there was silence in the room broken only by the sound of deep asthmatic breathing.

From the window the view across the sloping lawns of Nakasero Lodge extended beyond the trees to the wooded slopes of the hills that surround Kampala, where red-tiled roofs of pink, white and green villas nestled among the vegetation. Below them the minarets of mosques and the upper storeys of office blocks and modern hotels in the town centre were just visible. In the west the sun was beginning to set along the Masaka Road and the tin roofs of the mud-walled shanties that ran far out into the bush were glinting in its golden rays. It was a picture, if a misleading one, of a peaceful and attractive African town at dusk.

But from the throne in the President's office the view was different. Extending beyond the limits of the human eye it included an overall picture of the city and its defences, beginning at the extremities and moving in towards the centre.

All reliable elements in the Ugandan army, mostly southern Sudanese and the West Nile tribes, were concentrated in four units that ringed the approaches to Kampala. Thirteen miles north of the city the Malire Mechanised Battalion was stationed at Bombo, equipped with Soviet T–54 and T–55 tanks, armoured personnel carriers and scout cars. Near Jinja in the east was the First Battalion with tanks, 81 mm and 82 mm mortars, scout cars and A.P.C.s. On the shores of Lake Victoria, at Masaka to the west of the city, Soviet surface-to-surface missiles mounted on amphibious craft and A.P.C.s were handled by the Suicide Regiment. And in Kampala itself marine units equipped with T–25 tanks, more A.P.C.s and surface-to-surface missiles were placed strategically about the city limits. Finally at the bottom of the Nakasero Lodge garden the trees concealed a ring of T–25 tanks, scout cars and A.P.C.s manned by loyal Kakwa and Palestinians, who formed the President's Praetorian Guard.

The 'view' was laid out, therefore, according to the principle that the most effective armaments should be kept in the hands of the most trusted personnel and, in order to reduce the possibility of other units acting against him, deployed in concentric circles around the President.

Without warning he stood up and came round the back of the great chair. Moving swiftly, at six foot four inches tall and weighing nearly twenty stones, the sudden displacement of the President's bulk shook the room. He went to the desk and swung himself into position behind it, reaching for two telephones at once.

'I want to see Brigadier Ali, Major Hussein and Colonel Juma in my office within the half hour.'

One telephone went down. Into the other he said: 'Get me U.B.C.' There was a short delay. His free hand drummed nervously on top of another 'phone. Then he was put through.

'Telephone is haywire . . . Hello Salid. I want to give you a short broadcast about the shooting in Kampala last night. "A joint military exercise" – as you were – "shooting exercise. Life President Amin, his wife Sarah and their daughter Marian also took part. The exercise, named 'the Capture of Johannesburg,' took place at Cape Town View. It was intended to demonstrate how Ugandan volunteer forces, led by a suicide section of the army, could fight under the supreme command of F.M. Idi Amin . . ." Wait, Salid.' He put the 'phone down and picked up the first one again.

'Get a message to Juma that when he comes he should bring a list of all Ugandan exiles living in the U.K. I want to see Major Boschenko – right away. I want to see him first, alone. I want to see Juma next, but not so the others spot him there. No, first Juma. Then Boschenko. Ask the Duty Sergeant to come in five minutes or ten, with tea and scones. The moment there is news of the coffee smugglers I want it brought to me personally.'

He picked up the second telephone and was re-connected at once. 'Hello, Salid. As you were. ". . . under the supreme command of F.M. Idi Amin, when the necessity arises for Uganda to liberate South Africa by force of arms. The exercise comprised of men and officers of the Ugandan army, police and prisons. Police women and prison girls also took part . . . About using girls as spies C-in-C Amin agrees with his wife Mrs. Sarah Amin that girls should not allow themselves to be used as spies or agents of Imperialists, however beautiful they may be . . ."' The President paused and then suddenly roared with laughter. 'End of message. Thank you, Salid. Broadcasting is a big responsibility, but I have faith in you.'

He put down the telephone and sat back, one arm sprawling across the top of his chair. The burst of activity had come to an end. For a few moments he remained without moving. The enormous head sank into his shoulders so that the thick black folds of fat around his neck doubled over the collar of his army shirt. From under a grim frown that creased the President's forehead and drew a deep crevice across the bridge of his nose, the dark suspicious eyes looked out at nothing, but saw everything.

## TWO

In the bar at the top of the Speke Hotel, which has long been the exclusive preserve of senior military men in Kampala, Major Mustafa Hussein was relaxing. Not off duty, because as a member of the State Research Bureau his work was never finished: just relaxing. He was drinking Johnny Walker, listening to the high-life jazz of the Congolese band and watched a pretty girl in a tight fuchsia dress doing a rumba, but he was still vigilant. He noted who talked or drank with whom and for how long, and who came and who left together. Without appearing to do so, he kept an eye on everyone in the room. It was his job and people knew it. Major Hussein was a Nubian. His skin was dark and he wore a little moustache and sunglasses. He liked the idea that people were afraid of him.

His first reaction on seeing two of the President's personal bodyguard walk into the bar was to look round for a victim and reach quietly inside his jacket to undo the flap of his shoulder holster in case of trouble. Then he noticed that they were coming towards him: he guessed they wanted information on where to find their man. He nodded to them. The soldiers told him bluntly to come with them immediately on the President's orders. He began to protest that there had been a mistake, but thought better of it. Slowly he rose to his feet. Carefully buttoning his Hepworth sports-coat, to show everyone that his fingers were not trembling, he set out across the floor escorted by the soldiers and, with a smile here and a casual wave there to acquaintances around the bar, left the room.

It was a brave performance, but it did not lighten the fear that lay now like a bad meal at the pit of his stomach. He knew better than to ask questions, but all the way out to Nakasero Lodge, as he sat in the back of the jeep pinned uncomfortably between the soldiers in their camouflage suits, black berets and goggles, he searched his memory for anything that he might have done recently to attract attention. It didn't even have to be something bad . . . he had been summoned and that was enough to put anyone, whatever their rank or status, in fear of their lives.

In the ante-room Major Hussein recognised the older man sitting on a sofa under an oil painting of a charging elephant as Brigadier Ali, an army officer since before the coup. Hussein knew that he was in charge of the recent drive to stop the smuggling of coffee out of Uganda, but he could not see the connection with himself. Yet clearly they had been called together. He looked for signs of fear in the other man and felt some relief when he found none.

Presently the door to the President's office opened and the two guards outside snapped to attention as the Russian, Boschenko, emerged looking rather perplexed and sweating heavily. He closed the door behind him, cutting off the good-natured bellow of the President's laughter that seemed to echo about his heels as he made a hasty exit. The door remained closed for the next five minutes.

The summons did not come in the way Major Hussein or Brigadier Ali had been expecting. A guard, who had been standing beside them since they arrived, merely indicated with a movement of his automatic weapon that they should get up. The lack of respect shown by the guard was not unusual or significant. He then ordered them to walk into the President's office, knocking first but not waiting for a reply. The two officers did as they were told, marching in step across the marble floor of the ante-room.

Major Hussein knocked firmly and threw open the door for his senior to pass through first, then he followed.

'Brigadier Ali, I am delighted you were able to come at my speedy command. I hope that I have not taken you from your important duties.' The President rose from behind his desk and came forward to meet them with hands outstretched and a broad smile spread across his genial features. He was in a good mood. It seemed to bode well. But the friendly greeting was extended to the Brigadier only. Major Hussein received no more than a cursory nod and once more he felt the fear creeping in his stomach.

'According to a report I have just received the coffee smugglers are finally apprehended in their canoes on Lake Victoria. Well done, Brigadier!'

'Thank you, Excellency.' He bent his head.

'The smugglers have been properly dealt with, that is the main thing. Now you are stepping up anti-smuggling operations until the emergency is over, and we can rest peacefully in our beds.

'They are bad selfish men who shoot at the helicopter patrol and kill and wound your soldiers. The helicopter is lost, but I am not blaming you; that was not your fault . . . helicopters and armed carriers are not what soldiers need to win a war. What matters is a rifle and how they shoot towards the enemy.'

The President paused and smiled at the Brigadier, 'If you find yourself in a dangerous situation, Ali, you try to defend yourself and that is why God gave us knowledge to produce things to defend ourselves with such as combat aircraft, helicopters, carriers and so forth. God gave us intelligence to defend ourselves and that is why we say God helps those who help themselves. That is the meaning of the saying.'

The President wrapped a hefty arm about Brigadier Ali's shoulders. 'Do not think that the record of all that you have done is lost. It is my intention to reward you . . .'

At that moment there was a gentle knock at the door and Colonel Juma stepped quietly into the room. The cruel animal face of the President's chief executioner, the man they called 'the butcher of Naguru Barracks,' was well known to the two officers. Major Hussein felt the blood drain from his heart. He was as good as dead: the only real question that remained was the method of his execution – the reason scarcely interested him any longer.

'I was just saying to the Brigadier how I am intending to reward him for good work against the smugglers by promoting him to be a general of Uganda's Armed Forces.

This is a happy moment for him.' The President hugged him closer and looked deliberately at Colonel Juma, whose expression did not change. He had small red-rimmed eyes and the lower half of his face, dominated by immense nostrils, looked as if it had been twisted up from the jaw like the snout of a rhinoceros. He moved slightly where he stood, no more than a swaying motion, as if he was testing the air.

'I am now completely changing the subject.' The President laughed and, letting his arm fall suddenly from the Brigadier's shoulders, walked over to his desk. "Another group of bad people is that of the exiles who, after staying out for a time, decide to come back to Uganda quietly with the aim of confusing and buying the money-minded people, to plant time bombs and other explosives to kill me. But I have nothing to do with making money. I am drawing the pay of a Major-General, just to set an example. As the saying goes, greed killed the hyena. I cannot die and I cannot fear anyone, unless it is God's wish that I should die.

'In London the exiles are plotting to kill me when I visit the Queen's Jubilee. I have received a letter from the British Government . . .' He picked up some papers from the desk and waved them at his audience. '. . . to inform that they are advising me not to come because they cannot promise to vouch for security. I do not accept these words. I am not concerned with the shortcomings of the British and their economic problems. The plotters do not frighten me, only I want an investigation carried out to reveal the names of the people who are involved, because the British are no longer able to solve their simplest problems. That is why I am sending you to London, Major Hussein.'

The Major, who had been considering whether to make a run for it in the hope of being shot, stood to attention and saluted; but he was unable to control the smile of relief that forced its way to his lips.

'This is no smiling matter, Major.' The President looked dangerously stern. 'I am sending you on a life or death suicide mission to mop up all opposition in the U.K. You will take two of your best men from State Research and leave tomorrow morning sharp. Colonel Juma of the Public Safety Unit will brief you, providing a list of names of suspicious people and so on and so forth. The British Government can have no reason for preventing Uganda from fulfilling its duty as a loyal and equal member of the Commonwealth. I am not afraid to come because I will have no guarantee of my security. These are merely routine precautions.'

Major Hussein saluted again and said, 'I am honoured to serve Uganda and your Excellency.' There was a pause. The Major was uncertain what to do next.

'Brigadier Ali is leaving now to receive his promotion.' The President came forward and shook the Brigadier's hand warmly. 'I am not concerned for the loss of the helicopter. I am not blaming you. I have said it is my intention to reward you. And I am a man who keeps his word. Goodbye, "General" Ali.'

The Brigadier saluted proudly and mumbling his thanks quickly left the room. Major Hussein caught his eye as he passed and still saw there no sign of fear. The Brigadier was a fool, Hussein thought. He did not try to warn him; it was already too late. Everything, he saw now, had been arranged beforehand.

## THREE

*London, Thursday, 7th April*

The three Ugandan exiles arriving at Heathrow from Nairobi early in the morning of Wednesday, 6th April, received courteous, even friendly treatment from the Customs Officials and Immigration Authority at the airport. They were taken to a reception lounge on an upper floor of No. 3 Terminal Building and over cups of tea and biscuits were asked a number of questions by the Home Office representative. He asked them their professions, marital status, how much money they had with them, whether they had relatives still in Uganda, what their tribal affinities were, and how they had escaped from Uganda into Kenya. They gave satisfactory answers to all these questions and presented a number of convincingly horrific scenes of persecution, torture and mutilation, which their spokesman assured his listeners gave 'an everyday picture of Amin's Uganda.' The officials believed them and were sympathetic.

The only anomaly which struck the man from the Home Office was that the men all claimed to be members of the Basoga tribe, an affiliate of the Baganda. In his limited experience from interviewing a number of Ugandans coming to this country, he seemed to remember that the Basoga were fairly light-skinned people from the south, while these men were unquestionably very black indeed. They reminded him more of descriptions he'd read of Nubians and the West Nile tribes, though he'd never actually seen any himself: perhaps that was because they had less reason to flee Uganda than others. But he put any suspicion that he might have had firmly from his mind in case he was merely allowing prejudice to cloud his judgment. After issuing the Ugandans with thirty-day visitor's permits, he made an appointment with their spokesman to come and see him about extending their visas and applying for political asylum. He had been left in no doubt that should they return to Uganda, they would all be slaughtered.

Later the man from the Home Office answered some questions put by the man from Special Branch, Ports, who subsequently filed a routine report in triplicate which did little more than add three fictitious names to the list of Ugandan exiles living in Britain. By the time the report reached the desk of Inspector Loveridge, who anyway saw nothing unusual about it, the Nubians had long since sunk beneath the surface into the anonymous depths of the capital.

The Britmore Hotel is one of those dreary-looking establishments on the Cromwell Road, where only the most innocent or ill-prepared tourist gets trapped. Major Hussein had chosen it deliberately. From a tactical point of view it had many advantages, including a back exit that was accessible from the first bedroom floor. It had served him well once before.

Until the summer of 1976, when Britain broke off diplomatic relations with Uganda after the murder of the Israeli,

Mrs. Bloch, the Major had been attached in an unofficial capacity to the High Commission in London. He had lived at the Britmore.

He was glad to be back in London. He prided himself on knowing his way around the city and did not doubt that this was one of the main reasons the President had selected him for this important job. Finding two men from the S.R.B. with similar experience of the U.K. had proved difficult and in the end he had simply chosen his two best agents. One of them had been to Britain before, but that was only a brief visit to Stansted on a 'shopping trip' in the Lockheed Hercules which left Entebbe every Tuesday and Thursday to pick up luxury goods for the S.R.B. and some of the more privileged army officers. The second man had never been out of Uganda, but he had other talents.

They sat in the hotel's Crystal Lounge waiting for the Major, two large and silent blue-black men newly outfitted in Hepworth suits, floral shirts and light coloured platform shoes. The clothes they had brought with them had been more in keeping with their refugee status, but these had been discarded as soon as it was safe to do so. One of their first priorities had been a shopping expedition. Now they were back in uniform and ready for work.

Both men had pronounced tribal scars on their faces. The three slashes across each cheekbone looked like a sergeant-major's stripes – the reason that Nubians were always known by British soldiers as 'One-Elevens.' They had no proper names. As is often the case with low-born Nubians, the two men were distinguished by their epithets, 'Teenager' and 'Pair of Glasses.'

'Teenager' had earned his title in a previous decade. He was past forty now, with a wooden face and pock-marked skin that had a sheen like emery paper. A heavy man, powerfully built, he possessed a quiet ancient dignity that inspired respect. To use his name would have seemed like taking a dangerous liberty.

His companion, the one who had travelled to Stansted, was better suited to his nickname. There was no difficulty in distinguishing 'Pair of Glasses,' They were big old-fashioned frames in clear pink plastic with thick pebble lenses that had a white sheen at the edges and magnified the eyes in an alarming way. The face behind them was continuously smiling, the face of an easy-going country schoolmaster, open and friendly on first impression, until the ruthless glaze of his stare suggested a more sinister profession. 'Pair of Glasses' had realised a definition of happiness. His work was also his hobby. He killed for pleasure.

Beside his henchmen Major Hussein appeared young and somehow insubstantial. As he joined them now in the Crystal Lounge, he was forced to establish his rank by sitting slightly apart. They were drinking beer. He ordered a Johnny Walker.

Since morning he had been holding meetings with representatives of Uganda's interests in London. He had also spoken to Juma in Kampala. None of them had been much help. But an hour ago he had talked to an old friend from his High Commission days, who always knew everything that was going on among the exiles. His contact had heard nothing specific, but mentioned the names of faces that had dropped out of circulation recently without good reason. One of the names Major Hussein recognised. He found it again on the dossier that Juma had given him. It was under the section headed 'Relations of known enemies of Uganda.' A case of a brother whose name was on a list found in the possession of a foreign journalist and spy. A brother who was later executed for threatening to overthrow the President. The rest of the family had been removed. Sole survivor, therefore; settled permanently in U.K.; status, single; last address, etc., all the details were there . . . it hardly amounted to a striking coincidence, but it seemed as good a place as any to begin.

Major Hussein finished his drink and looked at his watch. He nodded to the other two, who rose to their feet and followed him from the bar, their new shoes squeaking as they walked. A moment later the three Nubians stepped out of the Britmore into the Cromwell Road and were swallowed up by the night.

# FOUR

'I can't hear.' The noise of the water running drowned his voice. She turned off the tap and opened the door into the sitting room.

'I just said, I am going to bed now.' He was standing by the sofa, clutching a copy of the *Financial Times* and a tumbler of whisky. In his blue silk pyjamas he looked rather vulnerable and sweet, she thought, like a little boy.

'I won't be long, I promise.' She came over to him and putting her arms around his neck kissed him on the cheek. 'It was a fantastic day. I want to thank you specially. You're so good to me. You know, I really can do it now. Solo, that's my new name – Solo Utegi, Queen of the Skies.' She laughed and rubbed her neck. 'I'm stiff. Golf Alpha Zebra Romeo. So stiff. I'll see you in a little while, O.K.?'

She kissed him and he patted her waist and said she was the best pupil he'd ever had. There was promise in the air between them. Nothing very insistent. A little musk. But it was there.

Ruth closed the door of the bathroom and turned the taps back on. The water cascaded into the tub and raised foam on the oily green water. She undressed slowly, sitting on the chair to pull off her boots, and then, because she was tired, wriggling out of her jeans and knickers without bothering to get up. She let them stay on the floor where they fell. Putting her hands behind her back she unfastened her bra and pulled it, along with her T-shirt and sweater, over her head. She stood up, catching a glimpse of herself in the long half-steamed mirror as she bent over to test the water with her hand. The contrast between the cool foam and the hot smooth water below made her gasp. A frisson passed through her body. She shuddered. Looking down at herself she noticed that her nipples had stiffened and were standing out from her breasts. If only Julian was a bit more – a bit less . . . but tonight she would be special for him. She lowered herself slowly, slowly into the bath. She thought of Michael but at once put him from her mind.

Lying back in the luxurious heat, watching the foam icebergs float the length of her long brown body, Ruth began to relax.

As the aches and tensions evaporated, she relived her triumphant afternoon in the sky. She'd done thirty hours solo. She could really fly. Julian was a true darling. He never once asked her about money . . . the line of thought led her back to the friends. She was meant to be attending a meeting tonight at the pub, but she'd felt too tired. The friends were not what she wanted to think about now. Tonight she was going to concentrate on teaching her flying instructor how to really take off. She smiled.

The sponge lay between her legs. She felt the heavy, saturated shape drift gently against her. Taking it with one hand she pulled it over her dark mound and squeezed hard so that the hot water was suddenly forced from the sponge directly on to her pubis. The action sent little shoots of pleasure darting through all her limbs and she repeated it until it seemed dangerous to go on. She closed her eyes and this time when Michael came into her thoughts, she did not banish him immediately. She felt relaxed and secure enough to be lenient on herself.

Ruth reached forward and turned on the tap for more hot water, then lay back. She could hear Julian moving about in the sitting room. He called out. She turned off the tap. 'What?' No reply. 'I can't hear you. Come into the bathroom.' He must have gone back to bed. She lay back again.

Behind her head the door opened very slowly. A hand reached inside and pulled the switch string, plunging the bathroom into darkness.

'Julian!' Ruth gave a little cry and quickly turned around in the water. 'What are you trying to do, scare me half to death?' She was playful, laughing and splashing. Then she went quiet to see if he was in the room with her. She heard breathing and the sound of creaking shoe leather . . . but that couldn't be right. Julian was in his pyjamas.

The scream never reached her lips. A hand came over her and pushed her down under the surface, holding her easily as she struggled and fought and the air in her lungs was gradually replaced by warm soapy water.

Major Hussein sat on the sofa with a glass of whisky to which he had helped himself on arrival, admiring the naked body of the girl who lay coughing and retching at his feet. He kicked her and she rolled over with a groan. Then he kicked the white man, but he moved less. Teenager had overdone it. The blood was spattered all over his pyjamas and the wall too. It was dripping from his legs, making a stain on the carpet.

'Wake this man up and put him in the chair, while I attend to the girl. I want him to watch carefully, so he can learn how to treat this kind of woman.'

Teenager dragged Julian's body up into a sitting position and slapped his face until the eyes opened. His gaze was fixed in a look of horror. The Nubian twisted his head round and made him watch as the Major forced himself between Ruth's legs and continually beat her about the face with his fists while he raped her. Afterwards he stood up and laughed at Julian, while he slowly zipped his trousers in front of him. Then he sat down again on the sofa. He took a sip of whisky and with a casual gesture indicated to the others that he had finished with her now and that, if they wanted her, she was theirs.

'Mr. whoever-your-name? Blue pyjama,' the Major began in halting English, 'Why are you plotting bad things against our President?' Receiving no reply, he said angrily, 'Wake up, Pyjama. This is not time for sleeping. Wake him.'

Teenager slapped him, but there was no response. Julian was already dead. Knocked senseless earlier by the Major's fists, Ruth came to in time to see her flying instructor slumped sideways, with his head hanging loosely and one lifeless eye staring at her. She screamed and the Major kicked her and said to her in Swahili, 'It was you we wanted, not him.'

Ruth tried to cover herself. She wanted to crawl away, but the Major put his foot on her chest and kept it there. 'Pair of Glasses likes your body, but I must talk to you, so we shall combine operations.'

She looked up at the smiling figure in the pink spectacles. He seemed to absorb all the light in the room and bring it out again through his glasses. As he knelt down in front of her they flashed a hideous distortion of cruel, greedy eyes. Ruth felt desperately afraid.

'Please, don't let him hurt me,' she pleaded with the Major. ' I haven't done anything. I don't even know what you want with me.'

Pair of Glasses came closer, smiling like a dog, lifting a corner of his upper lip till the teeth showed and then dropping it. He put a hand over her thigh and began pinching the skin on the inside of her legs, until she cried out in pain.

'I can make him stop,' the Major said softly, 'if you choose to help us.' He still had his foot on her chest and now he added a little pressure. 'Ruth, Ruth, you must tell us everything. Who are your friends? Where are they now?'

She shut her eyes. Gradually she felt herself being pulled along the ground towards the man with the glasses. The pressure on her chest increased suddenly till it became difficult to breathe.

'Leave her there. You must not move her. Do it there, you pig, so I can talk to her.'

The pressure on her chest lifted all at once, but now Ruth could feel the weight of the man in the glasses as he pushed open her legs and let himself down on top of her. She didn't dare to look, for fear of meeting those dreadful eyes. It was better not to resist, she told herself; this part was not the worst and it would be over. The pain was suddenly excruciating. She felt her whole body heave with revulsion as he entered her. The frames of his glasses scraped against her cheek.

'All this for nothing. You're a stubborn girl. Tell me the names of the men in your group. Where are you meeting? Now tell me.'

Ruth was crying and praying aloud, but the Major hit her across the mouth and silenced her. He slapped the man too, just to encourage him in his exertions. He poked him as if he were a bull, laughing at his solitary frenzy.

'Teenager, you're next,' he called out as soon as the other man had finished, talking in Swahili for the girl's benefit. 'Ruth, we have got all the time in the world. You know your mother and father in Uganda are very fond of you. Mrs. Utegi said you were always a good girl at home.'

'My parents are dead,' she cried and spat blindly. Pair of Glasses stood up and kicked her twice. The Major waved him aside.

'Your parents are alive, but they will be dead very soon if you don't tell us everything. Three days ago they were taken from prison at Bombo, where they have been staying comfortably ever since your brother was foolish enough to try to kill our President. Now they are being taken to Naguru Barracks until further notice. Do you want them to die?'

Ruth tried not to listen to the Major's insinuating voice, but she wanted too much to believe what he was saying.

'I talked to your mother before leaving Uganda. Ruth, open your eyes. Listen to me. She said your brother Paul was wrong to do what he did. She said I must ask you to come home and stop all this foolishness. Tell me about the others, Ruth.'

'I don't know where they are,' she sobbed.

'Listen, I can pick up this telephone and talk to Kampala and within an hour your mother and father will die. They will die in a terrible fashion.'

Ruth cried uncontrollably. If she only told them the name of the pub, what would it matter? They would go there and find them gone. She wondered what time it was. If they were still there the friends would see them coming and escape. Michael would know. He would understand.

The Major sensed that she was coming round at last to his point of view. Bending down, he gently lifted her to her knees. Behind him the other two turned away as if they knew the entertainment was over. Teenager wore a disappointed frown.

'Tell me,' whispered Major Hussein, 'and I promise, you will see your mother and father again and be reunited with them in Uganda.'

## FIVE

At four minutes to eleven the barman called for last orders. There was still a crowd around the bar and after considering their resources Michael and Tobias decided against another drink. They'd already had rather more than they were used to and were sitting staring at the gold-flocked wallpaper behind the heads of an elegant young group of Moroccans, who were playing the fruit machine.

'Super Crazy Hold,' Tobias read aloud, pronouncing the words carefully.

Michael said nothing. In front of him lay a copy of the *Evening News* with the banner headline 'JIM BANS IDI.' The article made it less clear that anyone had been banned from anything. But it had given them all a nasty turn when they first saw it on the news stands. And it was a worry now that 'public opinion' could be built up into an instrument of pressure for keeping him out. The meeting had been another disaster. First Ruth not even bothering to turn up; then Schulz and Osaya had to have an argument, which ended in both of them storming off in opposite directions. And now Tobias was drunk.

The Moroccans, all moustaches and scent, in natty blazers and brightly coloured, open-necked shirts, were making a lot of noise. Tobias let his gaze drift away across the room looking for a more peaceful scene. He found a mirror with an old-fashioned advertisement for Dewar's Perth Whisky cut into the glass that reflected the whole length of the saloon bar. Red-hatted chandeliers, dark wood, kegs of sherry, glass partitions with leaded panes, a wood-carving of an enormous bunch of grapes. He smiled to himself. That was the name of the pub: 'The Bunch of Grapes . . .' and all those people. He saw the door open and close. A black man wearing good clothes and a really smart set of shoes had just stepped into the room. Tobias looked at Major Hussein and caught his eye in the mirror. They both smiled.

The cold air of the Brompton Road revived him. He let

go of the marble pillar outside the pub and followed Michael down the street. National Westminster Bank, Crane Kalman Gallery, Underwoods, Olofson, Michael Hogg, Lucie Clayton, Norway Food Centre . . . Tobias still hadn't got over the habit he'd brought with him from Uganda of having to read every sign, every shop name and advertisement he saw posted up anywhere. Maple's, Crown and Sceptre . . . Michael was not being very friendly, walking out in front like that.

As they passed the Brompton entrance to Knightsbridge Underground, already locked up for the night, Tobias shouted ahead to Michael, 'Are we going to take the tube train?' Michael turned round impatiently and waited for Tobias, who was laughing and weaving his way along the pavement, to catch up with him. There were still plenty of people about. He checked automatically for anyone who might be following them. No sign of their friend in the denim suit. He noticed three men, probably Africans, window-shopping fifty yards down the street and dismissed them as tourists.

They crossed the street at Scotch House corner and joined a small queue waiting at the 52 bus stop. A bus came almost immediately. Michael and Tobias found seats upstairs. Someone had scrawled 'This is a Jambo Jet' across the yellow panelling. Tobias read it aloud and shrieked with laughter. Michael was looking down into the street. As the bus pulled away from the kerb he saw the three Africans emerge from the narrow passage that leads on to Knightsbridge Green. One of them was wearing pink glasses, which drew his attention. The man looked up at the top deck of the moving bus and the thick lenses caught the light.

Michael watched them, standing by the bus stop admiring the kilts in the windows of Scotch House, until they were out of sight. He wanted to believe he'd made a mistake, but the coincidence was unsettling. He thought of getting off at the next stop and taking another route home, but that would mean walking. They'd spent the last of their money on the bus fares and Tobias was in poor shape for a hike. Also they might be safer in the bus. Safer! Was he becoming paranoid? They were tourists, probably from the

Sudan . . . What did it matter where they came from? It was just that he didn't like the way they looked. He thought of asking Tobias's advice, but Tobias was asleep.

He woke him before they reached their stop. Tobias groaned loudly and complained of a headache. Michael decided against revealing his fears. As they went downstairs he took a quick look back at Ladbroke Grove. There was no bus following and only one or two cars, none of which invited suspicion. He felt relieved. They crossed the road under the railway bridge, Michael keeping a careful eye on the traffic. Tobias was singing now and cavorting about the street. As they turned into Cambridge Gardens a taxi came round the corner and gave him a moment's doubt, but then it gathered speed and turned left into the Portobello Road. Tobias shook his fist after it for no reason.

The distinctive note of the taxi's engine faded quickly into the monotonous *thump, thump* of Reggae music coming from Acklam Hall. On their right the great concrete sweep of Westway cast a long shadow across the waste ground, where the market overflows on a Saturday. Underneath the massive pillars of the motorway a group of West Indian boys in sock hats were hanging out and throwing stones and tin cans at a stray cat that had climbed on to the roof of a community playhouse. One of them looked over the road and noticed Michael and Tobias.

'Hey mister, what you got in that briefcase?'

'Let's have a look,' shouted another, and the whole group began moving up the slope to head them off.

At that moment Tobias, who hadn't quite taken in the situation, suddenly became convinced of the need to run. He careered off down the road, leaving Michael either to follow or stay and talk his way out of trouble. Michael made up his mind to run, but too late. The youths surrounded him. Laughing and jostling, two of them held his arms while another took his briefcase and another reached inside his coat for his wallet. Over their heads he watched Tobias run across Portobello into Acklam Road. He was doing right, taking the short cut home. A moment later Michael saw the man with the pink glasses.

He stepped out of a doorway into the Portobello Road

and stood there looking back at him. With sudden dread Michael recognised the tribal scars on his cheeks. He tried to warn Tobias. 'One-elevens' he shouted after him, but his friend was already out of sight. Now the other two Nubians emerged from the street's shadows and after a moment's indecision all three turned and went after Tobias.

'You've got to let me go,' Michael screamed and struggled to get free. 'They're going to kill my friend. You can have the case, everything, but let me go. Please let me go.'

One of the boys got angry and hit him. 'You fuckin' shut up and speak slow. We havin' trouble understanding you, mister African. What's the big hurry? You got something in the briefcase? How come you got no money? Where's the fuckin' key, you fuckin' black Jerk-off?'

'Help me, someone,' Michael yelled. 'They'll kill him.'

Tobias left the pavement and lurched through the gates into the empty building site. Only another hundred yards to go. Ahead lay the corrugated iron hoardings that blocked off the end of Springbrook Road. The top sheets gleamed in the light from the motorway; below, and all around him, was darkness. He could hear the footsteps of his pursuers on the road behind. Why did they have to go robbing black people? He looked back and saw that the one out in front had reached the gates. He called back to him, thinking it was Michael. There was no answer, but the footsteps came on.

The ground was getting rough and Tobias had to slow down. His head was splitting and he wanted to throw up. He couldn't understand why Michael wasn't with him. It was so unlike Michael to leave him like this . . .

Tobias tripped over a hard rut of earth and fell heavily, striking his head against a stone. The blow stunned him and he lay for a few seconds watching his head orbit the rest of his body. It came spinning back to his shoulders and slowly he picked himself up. The footsteps had gone away. He could hear the alternating calls of a couple of shrikes and thought only that the sound reminded him of the country around the Zezibwa Falls. Then everything was quiet on the building site but for the muffled roar of the traffic overhead. Definitely he had imagined it all.

A whisper came out of the darkness. 'Why are you running away? We only want to talk to you.' Tobias swung around.

'Dada sent for you to come home.' It was another voice coming from behind him now. He turned again and saw the gleam of a *panga* raised in the night above twin reflections on a pair of glasses.

The sound of the police siren scattered the West Indians. They ran for cover as if they'd suddenly come under enemy fire. After a moment's consideration whether or not to wait for the police, Michael ran with them. It would take too long to explain and they'd probably book him anyway because he was black. He ran down Acklam Road in the direction Tobias and the Nubians had taken. As he reached the gates of the building he heard the police car screech to a halt at the top of the street. He shouted back to them for help and set off again towards the hoardings.

Michael would have missed Tobias's body in the dark, but the police beam picked it up a few yards in front of him. The sight that met his eyes almost stopped his heart. Tobias lay on a heap of rubble with his head tilted back at an impossible angle. Underneath the Makerere beard, of which he'd been so proud, a deep gash glistened in his throat, where blood still pumped from the severed arteries and leaked hopelessly on to the ground.

Michael wanted to go to him, but close behind he could hear the police telling him to stay where he was. Now more than ever he could not afford to be caught. He ran to the gap in the hoardings and climbed through into Swinbrook Road. From there it was only a few yards to the front porch of their house. He got his latch key out as he mounted the steps and was inside the door before anyone reached the hoarding.

He watched through the letterbox as a policeman appeared in the gap, climbed through, then ran down the street and after a few minutes came back again. Michael hesitated, then went upstairs to pack a suitcase.

After getting no reply from the bell he let himself into

Ruth's flat on Holland Park with the set of keys she'd left with him in case of emergency. He turned on the lights and went into the sitting room, dreading what he would find, but hardly prepared for the scene of slaughter that confronted him.

The room had been systematically wrecked; furniture broken, carpets and curtains slashed, bottles, books, papers, pictures, lamps, objects of any kind – all swept on to the floor and piled up in the middle of the room. On top of the heap lay what had once been a corpse, now reduced to bloody segments of limbs that had been hacked off at the joints and cut again and trimmed like butcher's meat. The head had rolled on to the floor and lay behind the sofa. At first Michael thought that several people had been killed, there was so much blood everywhere. The walls, the ceiling, the doors, the fireplace, even the windows were spattered with it – as if there had been an explosion in the room. But then he saw that sections of blue pyjama and white skin were to be found on most of the blood-stained segments and he realised that if not the blood, then at any rate the limbs all belonged to one man. It meant that they'd taken her, whether dead or alive.

Michael stood by the door, his hand still on the light switch, transfixed by loathing and fear. He forced himself to cross the floor and open the door to the bedroom. He turned on the light. Everything was normal, untouched. The covers of the bed were thrown back and a copy of the *Financial Times*, under a glass full of amber-coloured liquid with half-melted cubes of ice floating in it, lay on the bedside table. He could see a black corner of Ruth's Bible sticking out from under her pillow where she always kept it. The contrast between the two rooms made him laugh aloud. Then he began to sob uncontrollably and falling down on his knees in front of the bed, he buried his face in his hands.

A slight movement in the next room brought him to his feet in an instant. Quietly taking up a pair of scissors from the dressing table, he crossed to the door, half expecting to find the Nubians had returned. The room was as empty as before. He tried the door to the bathroom. It was locked.

'Ruth, are you in there? It's all right, it's me. Open the door. Ruth!'

There was no reply. He tried the handle again and rattled it. 'Ruth, it's all right. Don't worry, nobody can hurt you. But we must leave here. Now, together, you and me . . .'

He heard a faint whimpering noise from the other side of the door. His heart beat furiously. Presently the key turned in the lock and the door opened.

Ruth stood there wrapped in a towel, shivering from cold and fear, staring out at him blankly with wide, terrified eyes. He moved towards her and put his arms around her shoulders and held her to him. Her teeth were chattering and her skin was grey with cold. He saw that her face was swollen with darkening bruises. He turned her head so that she didn't have to look again at the sitting room.

'Can you get dressed, do you think?'

She nodded, but made no move to do so. 'I'll help you,' he said gently, and took the towel from her. The sight of her body brought tears starting to his eyes. The blood ran down her legs and the bruises and lacerations covered every part of her. It was all he could do not to cry out, but he smiled at her. 'Come on, we'll find some warm clothes in the bedroom.'

When he'd done his best to clothe her, relying mostly on jerseys and a heavy winter coat, he took handfuls of her things from the drawers and filled a suitcase. As they passed again through the blood-spattered room, he held her head to his chest. She didn't speak until they were outside the flat.

'Where are we going? Julian never hurt anyone. He was kind.'

'We'll go to Osaya. He'll be able to help us. You never said anything about him to anyone, did you?'

She shook her head. 'I didn't mean to tell them. It was just the pub. The name of the pub.'

'I understand,' Michael said gently, trying not to think of Tobias. 'You did right.'

## SIX

Commander Bill Moffet looked up from the report on his desk and tapped the side of his jaw with a pencil. Tufts of hair grew on his cheekbones and the pencil gravitated there. He preened them thoughtfully, flicking the pencil upwards with a practised movement. His face looked particularly grey and the elephant eyes rolled menacingly.

'Loveridge, it isn't good. It's not what I want to hear from you. These people must be found. I don't like butchers and I don't like the idea of killer squads being sent over here and being able to go about their foul business as if it was the easiest thing in the world.'

'If you don't mind my saying so, sir, it was the Branch man at Heathrow who should have been . . .' Inspector Loveridge faltered.

'I know where to apportion blame, Arthur. I don't need your help for that. What I want from you is those three apes brought in and quickly.'

'It's going to be difficult to find them, very difficult. You know what they say about them all looking alike . . . Wogs I mean.'

Moffet groaned. 'These men are Nubians, Arthur. They are pitch-black, over six feet tall, built like trams, with tribal scars on their cheeks and one of them is wearing a set of luminous pink specs, goggles, gig-lamps . . . masters of disguise they are not. They probably don't know this country very well and it's doubtful whether they will have Embassy support from the Arab lot. They'll be sitting in some hotel or boarding house. I want you to check them all.

'Come off it, Bill. You know that's not on. If you want to put the whole of the C.I.D. in amongst it . . .'

'"In amongst it" is the word. Particularly felicitous Arthur. I thought Notting Hill C.I.D. were meant to know about the occupants of 120 Swinbrook Road. To be keeping an eye on our friendly exiles, instead of standing by while one of them gets killed, and then chasing the other halfwa around London as a murder suspect. Have you told them to lay off?'

'Yes, sir. But it was dark . . . May I ask if "Plover" has reported their whereabouts?'

Commander Moffet looked at his watch. 'The call should be coming through any minute now.'

'I suppose you could say, surveillance pays.'

'Possibly, Arthur. Remember the Palestinian in the denim suit? The Black Septemberist in the pay of the K.G.B., who turned out to be one of your lads after all . . .?'

'That is grossly unfair,' Loveridge protested. 'It was you who said all that about the K.G.B.!'

'One of your lads, and you tell me there was no question of C.I.D. surveillance. Arthur, this whole business is getting seriously out of hand. People are being killed and chopped about and we're running around with our pants down like something that escaped from a Brian Rix farce. I want you to go after the villains, Arthur, and apprehend them. It's what you know about, so get on with it.'

Inspector Loveridge rose to his feet and pulled on a brand new sporting trilby. He had a dogged expression on his face and looked, Commander Moffet thought, more like a policeman than it was good for any man to look.

At twelve-thirty precisely the green telephone rang. In anticipation Moffet had already moved his wife and children aside. They were grinning at him powerfully from the other end of the desk. He picked up the receiver and waited for the pips to clear.

'Plover here.'

'Good morning, Plover. What's new?'

'They've moved into Drayton Gardens.'

'Have they?' Moffet sounded impressed.

'There was opposition, of course, to the idea of letting somebody else in on their project, but they had little choice. The girl is finding it difficult . . .'

'Has Schulz moved in too?'

'Not for the moment. He'll stay in Willesden until nearer the date.'

'Any more trouble with the visitors from overseas? Or the boys in blue, for that matter?'

'No sign of anything yet. But it's pretty tense. There's very little talk about Operation Hippo. I'm afraid they're thoroughly demoralised. No-one thinks he'll come. They all suspect each other of being informers. Fear, I think, has intensified tribal and religious differences . . .'

'I didn't know you were an anthropologist, Plover.'

'A lot of argument, accusations being flung around . . . Ruth is still in a bad shape, but at least there has been a sort of rapprochement between her and Michael. But they're afraid. No one goes out, hardly. Guess who has to do all the shopping? But at least they're armed now. Schulz was finally persuaded to lend out some of his weapons. He's a nasty piece of work, by the sound of it – drinks too much. He could also be about to let them down pretty badly. Any chance of getting him out and replacing him with one of our own people?'

'Absolutely none and well you know it.' Moffet raised his voice in indignation. 'Whatever the stakes, Plover, we do not go in for government-sponsored assassination in this country. Abroad perhaps we may take a few liberties, but not here. I shouldn't have to remind you that it will not help you or your work to become too involved. You have a watching brief, Plover. Nothing more. So don't go getting any clever ideas.'

'All right, keep your hair on.'

'Any impertinence will go down on your record.'

'Not that one, if you're sensible, sir. Think about it.'

'Don't call me "sir" on this line.'

'Sorry, Bill!'

'The way things look the fat man may well not be gracing these shores in June. As soon as I know that for certain, I'll be bringing you in, Plover. And I'll see that your next assignment is a right one. Anything more to tell me? I'm a busy man.'

'So am I,' said Plover and the line went dead.

# SEVEN

At eleven a.m. on the morning of 22nd April, shortly after landing at Heathrow Airport, Lord Thompson, the former Commonwealth Relations Secretary, was driven directly to No. 10 Downing Street for private talks with the Prime Minister. He had just returned from a tour of Commonwealth countries as Mr. Callaghan's personal emissary. Ostensibly the purpose of his trip had been to discuss the Conference agenda with Commonwealth Heads of State, but a more important and sensitive task had been to sound out Commonwealth countries about President Amin of Uganda's proposal to attend the Conference and, if possible, to find support for the British view that, after the recent mass murders and bloodshed in Uganda, it would be intolerable if he came.

The Government was well aware of the risk of upsetting African states by seeking to ban an African leader, who had recently been President of the Organisation of African Unity. Its policy, therefore, had been to proceed slowly and with caution in the hope that in the end President Amin – who missed the last two Commonwealth Conferences in Ottawa and Jamaica in 1973 and 1975 – would himself decide, probably at the last moment, not to come to London in June. However, if the feeling among Commonwealth countries was preponderantly against allowing Amin to come – although no constitutional mechanism exists in the Commonwealth for expulsion of a member state – the British Government would at least feel on safer ground when taking a decision nearer the time on whether or not to bar him. Even so, the situation would remain delicate. And as a non-committal Lord Thompson told the press, when he finally emerged from No. 10, after being closeted with the Prime Minister for more than an hour, discussions with the Commonwealth countries would be going on for some time yet.

The intelligence that Lord Thompson had brought back

from his 'soundings' mission was relayed by Mr. Callaghan at a later meeting that afternoon in Downing Street to the Foreign Secretary, Dr. David Owen, and the Home Secretary, Mr. Merlyn Rees. From Britain's point of view it was not good news. The African leaders, although willing to condemn Amin in private, would feel obliged to continue to defend him from public reprobation. Some had criticised Britain as host country for trying to impose a precedent which was in reality an embarrassing attempt at re-establishing her former colonial relationship with Africa. Others had accused Britain of having a 'holier-than-thou' attitude towards Uganda. After all, did we not recognise Amin within days of the overthrow of President Obote and soon after entertain him handsomely at Buckingham Palace and No. 10 Downing Street?

'Of course,' the Prime Minister reminded his colleagues, 'it was a Conservative administration at the time. But the Africans have got a point. If we had been a bit more discerning then, Amin might not be the problem he is today. Tanzania, Zambia and Kenya claim that they were speaking out against the brutalities of Amin's régime six years ago, while we were calling him "Big Daddy," and laughing at the antics of a black buffoon. It's something I've always been against – this business of treating the man as a joke. He is not a joke.'

'Nor is the situation that faces the Government, Prime Minister,' the Home Secretary said gravely. 'Since it is clear now that there will be no unilateral move to ban him, this leaves us with the option of turning him back at Heathrow as *persona non grata* and simply refusing to let him into the country, or leaving it to chance that he will make his own decision not to come.'

'The former would mean an unprecedented international incident,' said Dr. Owen. 'It would be seen as a deliberate insult to an African Head of State, which the other African leaders would surely find very difficult to take. I doubt very much they would go on with the Conference in those circumstances, or even come to it in the first place, if they knew beforehand that was our intention. After all, in the past we have received as guests of this country, world leaders whose records bear invidious comparison with Amin's. The only difference is that they were more important on the world scene. But don't forget there are still more than two hundred British people living in Uganda. Their fate will hang in the balance if Amin takes the insult of being turned away at Heathrow the way I think he'll take it.'

'If we ban him . . .' the Prime Minister paused. 'You're right, David, the Africans would walk out and the whole Conference would probably have to be abandoned. There would then be formal protests and the question inevitably arises whether the Commonwealth itself could survive such an incident. Which leads us into pretty deep waters. One might argue that if our rejecting Amin on a point of principle leads to the break-up of the Commonwealth, the association is anyway no longer worth belonging to. Could this be the moment for Britain to withdraw?

'Don't think I'm advocating the break-up of the Commonwealth. I am not. But in my view it would be quite wrong to let Amin have his way. The Commonwealth must take the consequences of Britain's decision whom to admit to her shores. We are after all a sovereign nation. And remember, nothing would please the Russians more than to see Amin come to London and humiliate Britain by making a farce of both the Commonwealth and the Queen's Jubilee Celebrations.'

'But if we keep him out the Russians will profit equally by turning the rancour of every Commonwealth African country to their advantage and against us.' Dr. Owen leaned forward. 'When I discussed the problem of Amin with Mr. Shridath Ramphal, the Commonwealth Secretary-General, he advised me that some members of the Commonwealth have pointed out that it might be educational for President Amin to come to London to find out what other Heads of State think of his régime. A hostile press, the cold-shoulder treatment from his colleagues around the conference table and perhaps in private some blunt speaking from those with nothing to lose by it, could cut that man down to size. And that surely would be a small triumph for the Commonwealth and the traditions it has inherited from British democracy. We can't throw it all away because of one man.'

The Prime Minister took off his glasses and rubbed them on his knee, looking wearily at the two cabinet ministers. 'I don't mind admitting to you that I find it a very awkward situation indeed. Whether he comes or is banned it will be most embarrassing for H.M. the Queen and in Jubilee year that could make Britain look utterly ridiculous in the eyes of the world. Our best hope remains that he will decide himself not to come. And we must use every possible means at our disposal to encourage him in that decision. Private pressures have worked before with Amin. Over the Dennis Hills case the quiet intervention of Zaire and other African states had a lot to do with his being released, my own visit notwithstanding. I have discussed with Lord Thompson the best way of going about this and, David, you and I will get together with him later in the week and take that further.'

'The other line of approach is the security angle,' Merlyn Rees suggested doubtfully. 'The warnings we passed on through Ugandan officials attached to the Saudi Arabian embassy have not worked. Special Branch have reason to believe that Amin has reacted by simply sending a killer squad over here to clean up among the Ugandan exiles. It is more than likely that they have already killed two people. Of course the Branch and C.I.D. are doing everything they can to pick up these men, but the situation requires careful handling. As you know, there is at least one group of exiles who are plotting seriously to assassinate him if he comes. I think we are fully justified now – we have given fair warning that we cannot be expected to guarantee his safety – in merely keeping an eye on their operations. However, I'm told they are not a very impressive lot and that success is unlikely.'

'I don't think this is a very profitable line of discussion, Merlyn,' the Prime Minister interrupted with a smile. 'Let's leave it here, gentlemen. I am not going to make any decisions until I have to. Amin's invitation to the Conference stands and cannot be withdrawn, and unless something unforeseen happens there is going to be no all-round decision to ban him. But we can keep him out on any technicality, if necessary. As I pointed out in the House the other day, it will do no harm to keep Amin guessing. If we keep him a little off balance, he won't have the chance to stir up trouble beforehand. I should prefer him to be wondering from now until June what the actual position will be when he arrives. That is why I want to leave the final decision until the very last moment.'

## *Part Four*

# A SWORDSMAN IN THE SKY

## ONE

*Monday, 6th June, Kampala*
At five a.m. two camouflaged Willis jeeps left State House by the front gate and set off at high speed in opposite directions. One was a routine patrol vehicle and would make a quick circuit of the city before returning to barracks. The other was driven by a gigantic figure crouched low over the steering wheel, wearing dark glasses and a forage cap pulled down over his forehead, and was bound no-one knew where.

Ten minutes later the second jeep screeched to a halt outside a large pink villa in the secluded suburb of Kibuli Hill. Dogs began to bark, lights came on and presently a small plump man in a dressing gown appeared at the door of his home. The soldier informed him in a low whisper that the President was waiting for him in the jeep. The man pulled the door to behind him and shuffled down the path through the fading scent of his night-flowering plants. It was still dark and the morning was cool. He yawned noisily, used by now to the President's impromptu calls.

A Ghanaian seer and mystic, qualified as a doctor of medicine at Madagascar University, Dr. Micah had come to General Amin's notice in 1971, after claiming that he prophesied the overthrow of Obote. Shortly afterwards he had been installed as the President's personal soothsayer and had been living off the fat of the land ever since.

He opened the flap of the jeep and climbed into the passenger seat. 'Greetings, your Excellency.'

'Last night about three o'clock . . . I have to tell you this, Dr. Micah, in strictest confidence.' The President tried to turn towards him, but it was difficult for him to manoeuvre in the space available.

'Naturally, your Excellency,' Dr. Micah said soothingly.

'I woke up and God was tapping me on the shoulder. I had seen a bright vision in the night sky. Very bright.' The President pointed up through the windscreen of the jeep in an agitated manner. 'God had been telling me to wake up pretty quick and I would see something great.'

'What did you see, Excellency?' The prophet carefully stifled a yawn.

'I saw a bright vision in the night sky resembling a swordsman on a horse. Actually I thought I better tell you this quite frankly. A swordsman in the sky. This is very important. I made my prayer and everything, but what is the meaning?'

Dr. Micah was silent. He crossed his legs and straightened the folds of his dressing gown. Then he sat completely still and closed his eyes. After a few moments he began to hum.

'I tell you what I am thinking,' the President broke out, no longer able to restrain his impatience, 'for your information. God has sent this message to me, General Amin, as in the telex. I think this is the situation he wanted to tell me. Whether or not I am being advised to go to London tomorrow. This is the first thing. I know the day when I am going to die. God has told me so. That is why I am not a coward. *And I know exactly who will be making something against me very soon.* But he will get punishment from God straight. This is why I cannot be afraid. My death is in the hands of God, not in the hands of anyone else. I am the swordsman in the sky. Do you understand, Dr. Micah? I am just explaining to you.'

The soothsayer, who had stopped humming to listen to the President's words, now felt able to pronounce. 'Your Excellency, this dream is certainly a good omen for your visit. While you are speaking I have been talking to the spirit of Prophet John from Ruwenzori, where he lies among the eternal snows of the Mountains of the Moon. John says you are a great warrior and a roving ambassador for peace and goodwill. Your journey will be blessed. The horse is a sign of strength . . .'

The President clapped his hands and, rubbing the palms

together, blew into his thumbs. 'Thank you, Dr. Micah. Don't think I want to tell you many stories because, if such things do happen, I will come and relate them to you.'

'Have your dreams ever let you down, Excellency?' The soothsayer was a little perplexed.

'Never once. But God wants those whose hearts are with him, not just their exterior. If you really believe in your heart, Dr. Micah, he will save you from any calamity. This is how I believe I shall fly to London.'

Dr. Micah inclined his head. 'May God speed your return, Excellency.'

'That is all. You may go now – in strictest confidence.'

The President smiled and turned the ignition of the jeep. As soon as the engine came to life he revved up furiously and jammed the shift into gear. By the time the prophet had girded up his dressing gown and started to climb from his seat the vehicle was already moving. He flopped out with a little cry on to the pavement and squatted there like an ancient bullfrog as the jeep roared off down the road into the yellow dawn. The stars had all but vanished from the sky.

The long U-shaped table in the cabinet room at State House was cleared in a moment. Minutes of the meeting, notepads, pencils, spectacles and boxes of matches were all snatched up from its polished surface and locked into red and gold despatch boxes. As a body the military government of Uganda rose to its feet and saluted its leader. The President had remained seated throughout the meeting, which was unusual for him, but now he stood for the first time and putting a foot on his chair, held up a hand with one finger wagging close by his head.

'This last point I make is absolutely clear. Point five. You must *love* your leader. Love is very important. In all countries they are loving their leaders. Everybody must be loved. You know I am quite a popular leader because I speak the truth. Everybody listens for me. That is why the people like me very much. If I have nothing to say I keep quiet. I am telling you this. It is very important to love your leader.'

The soldiers saluted again and withdrew, leaving their

President alone in the cabinet room. A large Japanese-made electric fan in the corner by the window began to rattle. He walked over to the wall and yanked the cord from its socket. There was a knock at the door and Colonel Juma entered quietly. He carried a slim briefcase which he unzipped and placed on the table. The President came forward and took from it a clear plastic folder of papers.

'These are the names? All of them?' He scanned the list, tapping a pencil against the plastic. 'How many members of cabinet does this leave?'

'More than half. Thirteen to be exact.' Colonel Juma lifted his long snout into the air.

'Take one more. No, one less. Nothing must happen until Wednesday night. By then I am already in London. You will give Salid the information on Thursday morning so it can go out on the twelve o'clock news. These were bad people, rotten completely, caught plotting to overthrow the President in his absence. They were quickly defeated by hundreds of loyal army officers who all love their leader very much. Tomorrow evening at nine o'clock, no, let's say Wednesday morning, my imminent departure can be announced.'

'What about General Kitembe?' Juma looked away, his red-rimmed eyes watering and making him blink.

'There will be no problem with him. I shall talk to him this afternoon.' The President laughed and slapped Colonel Juma's shoulder. 'But you must watch Major Boschenko and those other Russians. They are my friends but they are stupid men and may do the wrong thing by mistake.' He laughed again and clapped his hands. 'Do not forget my instructions regarding the British and American nationalists. These imperialists have many ways of infiltrating in order to come and ruin our country.' He paused and wiped his brow. 'I think that is all I have to say, Colonel Juma. I want you to follow the practice that I pursue. Understood?'

'Yes, Field Marshal,' the Nubian said softly.

A table had been laid for lunch in the shade of a striped awning, but it was not yet midday and the guests were still relaxing in the sunshine. Serenaded by a guitarist in a pink shirt, they sat comfortably in wicker basket chairs, drinking

Pimms and watching the children play on the long sloping lawns that ran down to the edge of Lake Victoria.

'I have fourteen children, eight boys and six girls. You see I am a very good marksman.' The President raised an imaginary rifle to his shoulders and roared with laughter. 'How many for you, General?'

'Oh, not so many. I have just four. These are my youngest two you are seeing playing with Mwenga.' General Baker Kitembe looked a little embarrassed and took a quick sip of his Pimms. At that moment a fight broke out among the children. After a brief scuffle a little boy in white trousers, the smallest of the group, retired hurt and began to wail loudly.

'Come on, General, that's one of yours.' The President jumped up. 'You and I will go and sort out his problems. We will leave the women to discuss politics.'

The President, who was wearing a light blue tropical worsted safari suit that made him look larger than ever, took the General by the arm and set off across the lawns towards the knot of squabbling children. Mrs. Sarah Amin and the General's wife looked up and smiled politely at the men, then putting their turbaned heads together, they continued a slightly less subdued discussion to the gentle plunking of the guitar.

'I am keeping Britain guessing about my movements, General, until the last minute. This is my policy. And in Uganda too. No one here, except yourself and those who are making the arrangements, knows anything about my plans. You notice I said nothing at the cabinet meeting.'

'I think you did wisely, but I am confident that everything will go smoothly in your absence . . .' The General hesitated, uncertain if he were striking the right note.

'It will go smoothly because I am leaving you in charge of the country, Baker. That is why I can go freely to London and eat dinner and luncheon with the Queen and have no worries. I have beaten all the plotters and now I have complete confidence in you.' The President squeezed the General's arm and laughed. 'We are not putting all our eggs in one place, for your information,' he added mysteriously.

They had reached the lakeside where the children were playing. The little boy in the white trousers came running up to his father, who scolded him for making such a noise. The boy promptly started to cry again.

'My dear General Kitembe, this is no way to talk to your children.' The President wagged his finger at the soldier, then bending down swept the little boy up into his arms. Immediately the caterwauling stopped. The President lifted the boy over his head and placed him on his shoulders.

'Now you are a great rider and I am your horse. What is your name?'

'Nathan,' he said.

The President began to run and the boy shrieked with laughter. Soon all the other children gathered round, following and laughing, pleading to be lifted too. General Kitembe stood by and applauded weakly.

'Is this pretty one your daughter, General?' The President reached out an enormous hand to a shy little girl not more than eight or nine years old wearing pigtails.

'Yes, Marshal. Her name is Sarah.'

'In honour of Mrs. Amin.' The President smiled and walked a little way with the General's two children. Then he said to them both, turning a little so that the General could hear, 'Nathan and Sarah, how would you like to come with me tomorrow and fly with me in an aeroplane all the way to London?'

## TWO

*London*

At two p.m. on the afternoon of Monday, 6th June, two days before the opening of the Commonwealth Conference, a telegram from Kampala arrived at Buckingham Palace. The following is the text of the message.

> 'H.M. Queen Elizabeth II of Great Britain and Head of the Commonwealth, Buckingham Palace, London.
>
> Your Majesty,
>
> I wish to state right from the start that I, as Life President of the Republic of Uganda and Commander-in-Chief of the Uganda Armed Forces, will definitely attend the Conference meetings as Head of a Sovereign State and an equal member of the Commonwealth. It appears

to me that the British Government seems to believe that her former colonies, which are members of the Commonwealth, are inferior and can only attend the meetings when the British Parliament accepts to invite such countries. This cannot be the case. I, personally, and the entire people of Uganda are not against the people of Great Britain. But your majesty must learn this: that it is better to employ those modern British persons who do not have a colonial mentality and prejudice. Uganda believes in mutual respect among states.

I am very sorry not to be attending your Thanksgiving Service in the Cathedral about 10.30 tomorrow morning. I was very much looking forward to riding with you in the carriage for your Jubilee Celebration, but unfortunately I have some pressing engagements that are keeping me in Uganda. My arrival is postponed, but I am advising you of my visit now so that you may have ample time to help you arrange all that is required for my comfortable stay in your country.

Your majesty, it is ardently hoped and expected that you will, through various agencies, arrange for me so that I can see and visit Scotland, Wales and Northern Ireland. I should like to tour Britain and use that chance to talk to these peoples who are struggling for self-determination and independence from your political and economic system. I should like to meet the leaders of these liberation movements, particularly in Scotland, because as a revolutionary leader myself I am prepared to give them some sound advice. I would also like to meet the British Asians whom I booted out of Uganda in September, 1972.

May I take this opportunity to thank your majesty once again for the excellent arrangements made during my visit to your country in 1971, for the luncheon in Buckingham Palace and for your kindness in providing me with a special plane to fly to Scotland. I very much enjoyed my stay in Scotland and other places I visited and I shall never forget the warm hospitality I received there. All these arrangements proved the strong friendly feeling that you personally, the Government and the people of Great Britain have towards us in Uganda. We can never forget the cordial relations that have existed between our two countries for so many years.

I wish to take this opportunity, your majesty, to inform all my fellow colleagues, Heads of State of the Commonwealth, through you, that as the British Empire does not now exist following the decolonisation of Britain's former overseas territories and the collapse of the British economy, which has made Britain unable to maintain the position of the leadership of the Commonwealth, I offer myself to be appointed Head of the Commonwealth. This is in view of the success of my economic revolution in Uganda.

The Commonwealth is like a club for me, and not very important, but I think that it would be very appropriate if my fellow heads of state agree, for the next Conference to take place in Kampala, which now has very modern and up-to-date conference facilities. If they appoint me as Head of the Commonwealth I will extend invitations to all countries, including Britain.

I want your majesty to be reassured that you have the best friends in Uganda. I personally will never forget you as my former C-in-C of the King's African Rifles. The entire people of Uganda will always remember the sound education which we received from the British expatriates and missionaries, and which has now enabled us to stand on our own and to administer the country effectively.

Please accept, your majesty, my humble apologies for not being able to attend your Jubilee Conference. It is my ardent desire that you will come to visit Uganda very soon. I give you assurances of my highest consideration and esteem.

His Excellency Al Haji Field-Marshal Dr. Idi Amin Dada, V.C., D.S.O., M.C., Life president of the Republic of Uganda and C-in-C of the Uganda Armed Forces.'

'Does it, or does it not, mean he's coming? That's all I want to know.' The Prime Minister, in shirt sleeves, waved a copy of the telegram at his tired and slightly embarrassed-looking colleagues. For a long moment there was silence in the Cabinet room. On this occasion Dr. Owen and Mr. Rees were accompanied by the Permanent Under-Secretaries of their departments, who sat stiffly beside them at the table and looked whenever possible to Mr. Ramphal, the Commonwealth Secretary General, for answers. As hesitant murmurings started up at the top end of the table, the Secretary General again took the lead.

'I don't think this is his final message. At the last two conferences we received a telegram only on the opening day, stating that he was not coming. And I expect and hope that he will do the same again. This telegram to H.M. the Queen seems to me to have two main purposes, which characteristically have been muddled and obscured by the usual ravings. Amin is protesting that Britain has not the right to exclude him from a Commonwealth Conference and the bombastic confirmation that he will 'definitely be coming,' I believe, has more to do with face-saving than actual intention. He finds a way out by excusing himself from the Cathedral ceremony . . .'

'Which is one hell of a relief for me,' the Home Secretary interrupted with an apologetic smile. 'The idea of Amin sitting in St. Paul's with the blood of Archbishop Luwum still fresh on his hands has been the one thing that most people found totally unacceptable about his visit. At least we are spared that.'

'Yes, I think it's safe to assume that he won't be here tomorrow,' Mr. Ramphal said cautiously, 'and I think the rest of the telegram with its references to "postponing my arrival" and a "tour of Britain" and finally the confused apology for not being able to attend "the Jubilee Conference" would indicate that this is more a proposal for a state visit some time in the future. Again it's a face-saver.'

'In short, you think the telegram means he is not coming?'

'Yes, I do, Prime Minister.'

'Good, and I agree with you,' Mr. Callaghan said bluffly and snatched off his glasses, making a movement to stuff them in the breast pocket of his coat, but remembering halfway through the gesture that he was only wearing a shirt. 'What action has been taken on this telegram?' He put his spectacles down on the blotting pad in front of him.

The Permanent Under-Secretary at the Foreign Office leaned forward and looked up the table. 'We put through a call on his private line at Government House, Entebbe, after being told in Kampala that he was there giving an intimate luncheon for a few friends . . . A man who described himself as his personal secretary said that President Amin would not be acknowledging any calls from "minor officials" at the Commonwealth Secretariat, the Foreign Office or even from the P.M. himself. Aparently he is not speaking to anybody in Britain except H.M. the Queen. He has let it be known that if she rings he will be glad to talk to her.'

'Out of the question, of course,' snapped the Prime Minister, and the silence around the table fully endorsed his view. 'I think we have no alternative, gentlemen, but to assume that he *is* coming, while knowing that he very probably won't. The situation in Africa – forgive me, Mr. Ramphal, but there is nothing particularly confidential about what I am going to say – is now such that Britain cannot risk offending the African Commonwealth States by banning Amin. This has been borne out by David Owen's recent trip. Among other things we simply cannot jeopardise the work that's been done on Rhodesia. The Commonwealth still has an important role to play in the preserving of world peace. Let us hope that Mr. Ramphal is right in his reading of the telegram. But if not, at least we shall be spared a spectacle at the Cathedral . . . as someone mentioned.'

'There is still the question of security, Prime Minister,' Mr. Rees said a little reproachfully. 'If we let him in we know there will be violent protests, not only in the House but in the streets.'

'Yes, Merlyn.' Mr. Callaghan gave his sunniest smile with just a glint of frost for the Home Secretary's benefit. 'You and I can discuss that one in a little while. But let's look on the bright side. I'll give ten to one on against his coming. Fair odds?'

'Fair dos,' said one of the Permanent Under-Secretaries. 'I'll have a fiver . . .' He traded the rest of his sentence for the promise of laughter, but it was not fulfilled.

'Our bets are all going the other way, John,' his Minister covered up hastily.

An embarrassed hush descended on the Cabinet room.

As he walked past 10 Downing Street the man in the leather coat smiled politely to the tourist who was trying to take a photograph of an unwilling child standing on the steps beside the policeman. He quickened his pace and held up a hand as he passed through the frame of the picture. The tourist waited till he was clear and then pressed the button. The man walked on unscathed.

In Whitehall Schulz turned right in front of the Cenotaph and came down Parliament Street whistling a tune that bore some resemblance to Offenbach's Can-Can Overture. On the corner of King Charles Street he stopped to buy an evening paper, which he stuffed in his coat pocket without even glancing at it, but pausing briefly to look across the street to the entrance to New Scotland Yard. Then he turned up King Charles Street and walked slowly back under the shadow of the Foreign Office towards St. James's Park.

Outside the main entrance to the Foreign Office he stood in the guise of a tourist and stared through the pillared archway into the quadrangle. He read the notices advising visitors that they would be asked to disclose the contents of parcels and personal baggage, that the maximum speed for cars is five m.p.h. and that all passes must be shown. The two uniformed men behind the wood and glass kiosk under the nearest arch looked out at him enquiringly and he stood back pretending to admire the wrought-iron gates with their little gilt crowns. Schulz listened to the sound of footsteps echoing across the quadrangle. He moved on at a leisurely pace, gazing up at the dirty windows and thinking how the whole building could do with a good clean, but carefully noting the iron mesh behind the dismal curtains. The place was a mausoleum. Not really his style. He felt sure now that he'd made the right decision.

He walked under the statue of Clive and ran down the steps into the sunlit park. He found a bench and sitting down beside an old man smoking a pipe, took out his paper. The headlines were still speculative. It was all right. He wondered what he would do now if the man actually came. His preparations were made, everything under control, beautifully planned down to the very last detail. But, of course, he was banking on not having to go through with it. If the man came, he smiled, it would be an exquisite irony to have planned the perfect attempt, to have taken so much trouble to get everything right, and then not to bother with completion. The Unfinished Symphony. Schulz laughed. And those stupid niggers who were so worried because he'd got a little too much to drink now and then.

The smell of the pipe tobacco irritated him. He jumped up, leaving the paper on the bench, and set off again whistling gaily. There was something faintly comic about the way he walked, and children turned and looked after him as he went by. It had to do with his legs being slightly bowed, which gave a seaman's roll to his gait. It was why, even in June, he preferred to wear his long leather coat.

The path he'd taken led round by the pond and brought him back to Horse Guards Parade. He stopped by the Guards' Monument and, turning his back to the parade ground, looked up at the four cast-iron statues. The soldiers' black bayonets glinted in the evening light. Schulz brought his gaze down to the level of the plinth. Immediately behind the monument he could just see the top of the border of red and white and blue flowers that grew up the bank as far as the line of bushes. Behind the greenery a wattle fence completed the screen. At the back of it lay the headquarters of the Royal Parks Constabulary. On Schulz's right an approach road led into the horseshoe compound, where there were offices, gardening sheds, a car park and a canteen – all completely hidden from view by the encircling bank of flowers. It was a successful piece of landscaping: from the parade ground the whole structure looked like a natural mound that had been turned into an attractive garden.

Schulz looked at it with an air of satisfaction. At least the British knew how to create a park. He smiled to himself and screwed up his eyes. Under the topmost of the bushes, on the edge of the cutting where the approach road curved into the attendance 'pit,' he could just make out the faint outline of the marker. It was still in place; so long as the good weather kept up, everything was going to be all right.

# THREE

*Tuesday, 7th June – London*

By 9.45 a.m. Commander Moffet was ready to go out. He stood by the window, considering the inviting green of the trees in St. James's Park, expecting the duty sergeant to announce his car at any moment. Dressed in a grey pin-striped suit, white stiff collar, pink tie and in his buttonhole a pink carnation, he looked almost tidy, but more than ever like an elephant. His bowler hat – a black Howdah – lay on the desk behind him. Moffet was in a bad mood. He hated functions; he hated having to leave the office at a time like this; and he hated the Deputy Assistant Commissioner. The green telephone rang. He picked it up and spoke first.

'Not now, Plover. I'm on my way out. Can't it wait? I've got ten minutes to get to St. Paul's.'

'You can turn on the siren – like Kojak.'

'Plover, I'm not in the mood for you. This had better be good. Have you found out anything?'

'Look, if *you* don't know whether he's coming, how are we supposed to know?'

'You understand perfectly well what I mean, Plover.' Moffet raised his voice.

'All right. No, I haven't. None of us has any idea. Schulz keeps his cards close to his chest. Maybe he's got nothing in his hand.'

'This really is a bloody nuisance. The whole reason for your existence, Plover, is to find out how and when . . before, rather than after it happens.'

'We didn't reckon on Schulz. Anyway he's moved into Drayton Gardens and from now on the others will be keeping a pretty close watch on him. They realise he may try to do a bunk with the money. I think he's just been counting on the fat man staying at home. Michael, for some reason, is still convinced he's coming.'

With his free hand Moffet lifted his bowler and glanced at the headlines of the terraced pile of newspapers that lay underneath. They ranged from 'PRESIDENT AMIN

POSTPONES VISIT' to 'IDI SENDS ROYAL REGRETS'; from 'JIM CALLS BIG DADDY'S BLUFF' to 'BANNED!' Only two papers sounded a note of caution in proclaiming Amin's visit to Britain for the 1977 Commonwealth Conference cancelled.

'So am I,' he said quietly.

'Sorry?'

'So am I convinced he's coming. But you can tell your friend Michael we find ourselves in a minority. I've got to go now, Plover. My presence, it seems, is needed at the Cathedral. For some reason more than half the Heads of State have decided to attend the service. A bomb in St. Paul's, it has been pointed out to me, would be more damaging to Commonwealth relations than anything friend Amin might have come up with. Past tense, you notice. I tried to disagree, but . . .'

'You don't sound yourself, Chief. I thought the Heads of State were mostly arriving tonight.'

'This is Jubilee, Plover. Everybody likes a parade. There's to be no ban, by the way. Do you understand? No ban. If he comes, then he's in. I've got to know the fat man over the past few months; I think he'll be here by tomorrow morning.'

'Christ.'

'Now the moment you get news of his arrival, I want you to report back with the reaction from the group. Schulz will have to make a move.'

'It'll be difficult, Chief, but I'll try.'

'And Plover . . .'

'Yes, Chief?'

'Don't call me Chief.'

Schulz had brought his own camp bed and set it up in a corner of the second spare room. There was no other furniture and a bare light bulb hung from the ceiling; the paint and paper were peeling off the walls. Sally Temple Owen's plans for decorating her flat had not matured in the past months. But the new tenant could put up with discomfort. He had all he needed, as he was fond of repeating. His transistor radio stood on the floor beside the bed and under the bed lay the three canvas sacks. A symphony by Schubert echoed around the bare walls.

'I think it's time you told us your plans, Schulz. It was never part of our agreement that you should be so secretive.' Michael spoke from the door, which he had closed behind him and was leaning against. Schulz lay on the camp bed in his underpants and a dirty white T-shirt. His hands were clasped behind his head and a cigarette hung from his lips, spilling ash on his chest.

'It was never part of our agreement that you should get yourself into such a position that you can hardly leave this flat.' He paused to remove the cigarette from his mouth. 'I can handle the police if I have to: I can handle Nubians. But I don't want to be compromised when I'm doing my job.'

'Of course not,' Michael smiled. 'It's just that it's getting close and we don't have any . . . well, some of us still favour the Hyde Park Hotel idea. I know Osaya does.'

'Then go ahead. I'm not stopping you. Here, I can even lend you a rifle. But don't ask me to have anything to do with it, because I know it won't succeed. Look, in a situation where there are so many uncertainties, you have to choose the moment of least doubt. That's what I have done. That's been my policy all along. When I joined this operation you had fifty goddam plans and none of them were going to work. Now I've got it down to just one. If he comes, it will stand a very good chance of success. You and the others will know what it is when you need to know, not before.'

'We've paid you five thousand pounds, Schulz, and we have nothing to show for it except you lying there with your gun and with too much drink inside you.'

'If you want me to complete the contract, you have to agree to my terms.' Schulz turned over and faced the wall.

'All right, because I have no choice, but you must make . . .' Michael couldn't finish his sentence. He left the room, slamming the door behind him. He stood in the long dark corridor listening to the sounds of Schulz's transistor and trying to control the rage that churned inside him. He'd been cooped up in this place for much too long. They were all suffering from it. Jumpy as cats. But it was up to him to keep things calm.

He took a couple of deep breaths and opened the door to the room he shared with Ruth. She was sitting with her back against the wall on the double mattress that lay on the floor in the corner furthest from the window. She was reading a flying manual. The sight of the book irritated Michael. It was all she ever did now – talk about flying or read those damned books. But he never said anything. She looked up at him and gave a distant smile.

He sat down beside her on the mattress. For a while neither of them spoke. Then he said, 'By this time tomorrow, we will know that it hasn't all been a waste of time. That Tobias didn't die for nothing . . .' He paused as the memory came back. 'After that it will be up to Schulz.'

Ruth put her hand on his. 'You must try and get some sleep tonight. You're beginning to look hollow-eyed, like a tired man.'

'Sleep!' Michael laughed harshly and struggled up from the mattress. He turned away from her and crossed to the window, which looked on to a featureless courtyard. Since the night of the Nubians he and Ruth had been a comfort to each other. They slept together in the same bed, and over the weeks that followed they had gradually fallen back into the gentle patterns of their old relationship. There was affection between them and an easy acceptance of intimacy, but it was a warmth now between brother and sister. They never made love together, or even talked about it.

Michael knew that Ruth had not recovered from her experience and he never let it be known that he wanted anything more from her at night than to hold her in his arms. When she screamed and struggled in her dreams, he soothed her. There was no question of his taking advantage. She seemed oblivious to his needs and in some ways it helped him to keep control. But lately, as the worry of their mission kept him awake night after night, it had become more difficult. The softness and warm smell of her body so close to his made him long to wake her and re-explore the mounds and crevices he knew so well with a new tumultuous passion. But shame held him back. Across the corridor the hot sounds of boisterous love-making coming from Sally and Osaya's room did not help matters in the least.

'Ruth, when this is all over, you and I . . .' Michael said

bravely, turning round from the window, but Ruth hadn't looked up. She was once more immersed in her flying manual. He thought better of what he'd been going to say. Instead he murmured softly to himself, 'Dear God, let that fat ugly bastard climb into the sky tonight and come.'

*Entebbe, 8.30 p.m.*

The Presidential jet, a bright red Executive Gulfstream, bearing the black, red and yellow insignia of Uganda Airlines, stood gleaming under the airport lights in front of the terminal building. American maintenance men were carrying out last-minute checks as the President's personal baggage, consisting of three trunks, seven hampers and five heavy suitcases, was being loaded under the careful direction of an S.R.B. security man. Thirty yards away across the scarred and pitted tarmac an elderly Boeing 707–320C had also been made ready for departure. Lined up for inspection under the shadow of its wing, in grass and barkcloth skirts with orange and red Idi Amin shirts, carrying spears and drums and a wide variety of musical instruments, two hundred men and women of the Heart Beat of Africa dance troupe were waiting for their leader. Television cameras stood by with battery lights; and a raised dais covered in microphones (many of them without leads) stood in front of the dancers. Soldiers ringed the approaches to the airport.

At the first sound of the approaching helicopter the Heart Beat of Africa began to thump. But the music was quickly drowned by the roar of the army chopper and the dancers had to continue their gyrations to the clatter of its engines, looking up in fear to the dark shadow in the sky that suddenly blotted out the stars. The beam of a searchlight fell from its belly and the helicopter began a slow descent to the ground, sending up strong gusts of wind that nearly carried off the costumes of the dance troupe. As soon as it touched down and the blades slowed, the women set up a loud squealing noise that was the traditional greeting for a great chief; military police in red-topped flat hats ran forward under the swirling screw to open the near-side passenger door; and to a thunder of drums, chanting and applause, the President stepped out on to the tarmac. With his hands clasped together over his head he made a victory run for the dais.

He stood in front of the barrage of microphones, dressed in his Field-Marshal's uniform festooned with medals, smiling at the TV cameras and the dancers under the wing of the Boeing, as he waited for the noise to die down. Without warning he drew a small revolver from the white plastic holster at his ample waist and fired it into the air. There was immediate silence.

'Fellow Ugandans, I am announcing my imminent departure for the U.K. to attend the Commonwealth Conference in London starting tomorrow at 10 a.m. sharp. All imperialist British attempts to "whitemail" me have failed. I shall be there on time to advise the Heads of State about my supersonic policies for the future of Uganda and the Commonwealth. This is my position. And for Ugandans I want to bring this to your attention. I am not making a speech because there is not time. But I am reminding you that the revolution in Uganda is most important.

'The revolution of Uganda will not stop whether I am here or in foreign parts, whether I am alive or not alive. I want to assure you that nobody will deceive you so as to overthrow me and bring another government. No. The government belongs to the members of the Uganda Armed Forces, not me. Whatever I am doing, I am following their policy. Therefore, if you are aiming at me you are deceiving yourselves. You are not deceiving me. And everybody should be very thankful to me and I am advising that you should not do anything.

'Many people have said Dr. Amin is a God-fearing man who has done many good things for the peoples of Uganda. Nothing will ever shake me from my objectives and determinations. Once while attending prayers in Al-Azhar I met a very old religious shaykh, who told me frankly from the bottom of his heart that God will always be on my side.

'There have been very many nasty incidents against my life. As a revolutionary leader and a progressive who is fighting for black peoples all over the world, I expect to have enemies, twenty-four hours a day. But I have always escaped miraculously.

'One incident during the September, 1972, guerilla invasion,

I was driving a jeep in Mutukula and the guerillas aimed at me, but their arms became so shaken that they could never pull the trigger. This is because I have divine protection.

'One day I was swimming in the river near the heavy quarters of hippos and crocodiles, and one crocodile captured me, dragging me over two kilometres under water, but once more God saved my life. There are millions of true stories like these . . .

'But I have no more time to say, only you must love your leader. This is very important. General Amin only speaks the truth. All people of Uganda must love him very much. Thank you.'

The Heart Beat of Africa cheered and stamped their feet on the ground and rattled their spears as the President stepped off the podium and walked towards the Gulfstream followed by a cluster of aides. Passing in front of the two-hundred-strong dance troupe, who were to accompany him to London, as he himself had widely advertised, the President stopped in front of a pigmy group from the Mountains of the Moon, known as the 'Dingi-Dingi' dancers. Bending down from his great height he shook hands and joked with them about their flight to the other side of the world. For the benefit of the TV cameras he reached out and seized a small ceremonial sword that one of the dancers wore on his belt, intending to hold it up to the crowd; but the gesture was hurried and the sword slipped from his hand and fell to the ground. The blade, made of cheap cast iron, shattered.

The pigmy let out a sharp cry and stepped back, holding up his hands in superstitious horror. Pieces of the sword had landed in a pool of water, disturbing the clear reflection of the starlit sky. At once the others cowered beside him and the whole group set up a low wailing sound. For a moment the President stood transfixed, staring down at the fragmented sword. Seeing that something was wrong, one of his aides quickly moved in front of the TV cameras, waving at them to stop filming. But the President had already regained his composure. Smiling broadly and waving to the dancers, he walked swiftly across the tarmac to the waiting jet.

Inside the Gulfstream those who were to accompany him

to London had already taken their seats. The President climbed aboard and eased his great bulk through the partition into his private compartment in the front of the plane. His own seating arrangements included a replica to scale of the great throne in his office at Nakasero Lodge. A safety belt had been attached to the mock buffalo horn armrests, but he did not bother to fasten it. As the plane taxied out on the runway, a stewardess in a turbaned headdress brought him a beer glass of Drambuie on a silver tray. As soon as she left the compartment Lieutenant Abdala came through for last-minute instructions.

'Get a message to the tower that I have changed my mind about the Heart Beat dancers. At a time of economic crisis Uganda cannot afford to waste precious fuel. The 707 will take off five minutes after we leave, do a couple of laps in the air, then return to base. Understood?'

'Yes, Excellency.'

'Are General Kitembe's children on board?'

'They are sleeping soundly, sir.'

'Good. If they wake up and are afraid, send them to see me and I will look after them.'

'Is that all, sir?'

'Yes, you order the pilot to take off now quickly.' The President drained the glass of Drambuie and handed it to his aide.

When the man had gone he put his feet up on the table in front of him and sat back comfortably in his flying throne. The high-pitched whine of the engines built up around his ears, then with a sudden lurch forward the plane began to speed down the runway. The President consulted his massive gold wristwatch. It was 9 p.m. exactly. He was on his way to London.

## FOUR

*Wednesday, 8th June – London*

It was Schulz who first heard the news on his transistor. He called the others in to listen; they crowded round the radio, hardly able to suppress their excitement, while it was announced in the calm detached accents of the B.B.C. that President Amin of Uganda had arrived at Heathrow at 10 a.m. that morning and, despite earlier hints that he might be banned from entering the country, had not been turned away. The friends clapped and cheered and kissed each other. Schulz had to restrain them to hear the rest.

'The last of the Commonwealth Heads of State to arrive, President Amin was met at the airport by officials from the Commonwealth Secretariat and representatives of Ugandan interests in Britain. He was then driven immediately to Lancaster House, where he arrived a few minutes late for the opening ceremony of the Commonwealth Conference.

'In spite of his promise to bring a 250-man delegation with him to London, including the Heart Beat of Africa dance troupe, the President's party was not unduly large. As he stepped off the plane, two pipers wearing kilts and glengarries played a familiar tune, which the President assured the two or three reporters still at the airport was called "Uganda the Brave." The President also said that he was happy to be back in Britain, which he regarded as his spiritual home. Dressed in a Field Marshal's . . .'

Schulz snapped off the radio and looked at the others. His mood was different from theirs. The grey eyes, more bloodshot than usual, narrowed till they matched the slant of his cheekbones. 'So he's come. Now "Operation Hippo," as you have chosen to call it, can proceed. But remember what I said. I have already selected the moment when the target will be correctly positioned. It means waiting a little longer. Don't spoil it by being impatient. This is the hardest time for everyone.' Schulz paused and drew in air importantly through his wide fleshy nostrils. 'But you can rest assured that there will be successful completion of the contract. I would suggest in the meantime that no-one leaves the flat . . . except for basic necessities.'

'That is completely ridiculous,' Osaya burst out. 'We are putting everything in one basket and we don't even know what it is. If you fail, Schulz, how many opportunities will we have missed? We must watch him now all the time and take any chance we can get. You stay here if you want to, but nobody can stop me from leaving this place.'

'I think you may be right,' Sally Temple Owen held her lover's arm. 'We should follow his movements. Something unexpected might happen . . .'

'Like being picked up by the police or Amin's goons,' Schulz sneered. 'Go ahead, if you want to compromise the whole bloody operation.'

Michael intervened tactfully. 'I think Schulz is right, Osaya. He is the expert and we have agreed to trust his professional judgment. It would be a complete disaster if one of us were to get caught now. Let's sit tightly and keep watch from here. We have Sally's TV, the radio and newspapers. We can learn more that way than from a hurried glimpse through the bullet-proof window of a limousine.'

'Why can't he throw a grenade?' Osaya looked stubbornly at Schulz.

'Because grenades don't always work, as previous attacks on your President have shown, because I don't have a grenade and because that is not my way.'

'He is *not* my President,' Osaya flared. 'Anyway, what about the plan for the Hyde Park Hotel? Is that to be jettisoned completely?'

'Osaya, look,' Michael said patiently, 'we've been through all this before. Really it's better if we stay here and everyone relaxes and waits. We should be happy for one thing and thank God for sending him to us. Don't worry, I promise you he will never return to Uganda.'

Osaya gave a short nod. 'I'm going out now –' the others looked at him – 'to buy cigarettes.'

The next forty-eight hours proved Schulz's and Michael's policy to be sound. Contrary to expectations President Amin kept a low profile during the first few days of his visit. The heavy schedule imposed by the Conference agenda as well as private debates, meetings and official functions laid on for the Heads of State by the Government left little time for any extra activities. Along with the other Commonwealth leaders he attended the Queen's banquet at Buckingham Palace on Wednesday night, where, according to newspaper reports, 'he conducted himself like a perfect gentleman.' The following evening he dined with the Prime Minister and afterwards watched the River Pageant and firework display from County Hall.

There were a number of demonstrations against his visit, organised by the Uganda Action Group, mostly well-intentioned liberals, who seemed disappointed by the small number of Ugandans who actually turned up to be counted on the day. Watching a *News at Ten* report of a protest-action outside Lancaster House, which ended in scuffles with the police and a number of arrests, the friends saw the reason for their absence. Amin's men were among the crowds.

A press conference given by the President in his suite at the Inn on the Park – a change of plan which had taken the conspirators by surprise – turned out to be a low-key affair. Amin was dressed flamboyantly enough in a bright green safari suit with a cravat and white stetson hat, but his speech was a dull rambling affair that went on for much too long. Many of his audience became restless and left before the end. There were fewer jokes than usual.

When asked about reports of mass murders in Uganda, President Amin replied: 'We are a most peaceful and protective state. Anyone in Uganda now can be sure of a safe future, protected with a good and sound army. There is complete confidence in my leadership, with no possible gambles or squabbles caused by a political upsurge that would waste a lot of time on argument . . . my policy is non-aligned, we have no mass murders. I love everybody completely . . .'

And more hostile or more awkward questions – on the death of Archbishop Luwum, for instance – he brushed aside without any attempt at giving answers. There was something subdued, even slightly pathetic about his performance, which Michael noticed at once from the brief clip shown on the news. He pointed it out to the others, but Osaya was still smarting over being shown up in the wrong about the Hyde Park Hotel and neither Schulz nor Sally thought it was significant.

'Perhaps he is suffering from jet-lag or ate something bad on the plane.'

'He has two food-tasters. No, there's something wrong. It's as if . . .'

'Another dose of the clap?' suggested Schulz crudely.

". . . he knows. I think he knows that he's going to die.'

# FIVE

*Friday, 10th June*

The green telephone on Commander Moffet's desk rang at 4.30 p.m. He snatched it up.

'Plover, where in the hell have you been? What's going on out there?'

'It's been tricky getting away from the house. Schulz has finally made his move.' The voice hesitated. 'At least he's let us know when and where.'

'Well?'

'Tomorrow at the Birthday Parade – Trooping the Colour or whatever you call it – on Horse Guards.'

'Where from? How's he going to do it? Come on, Plover.'

'All right, all right. He didn't give any details. Somebody has to pick him up afterwards in Petty France with the Mercedes at twenty to twelve.'

'That means after the Trooping. He must have said something else.'

'No. The others wanted to know more, but he wouldn't say. That's all there is.'

'Could it be a bluff? Do you think he's getting ready to run?'

'I did. I'm not so sure now. He seems to have pulled himself together since Wednesday. But he's still as cagey as ever. He might suspect me, or one of us, I don't know.'

'You'd better get back there and stay with him until you have something. Don't hang about. Any scrap of information, anything at all, I want it right away. We haven't got much time.'

'I thought we weren't going to interfere.' The voice sounded a little disappointed.

'Plover, I get my orders from above, the same as you. Now get on with it. I'll be staying at the office tonight. You can come through at any time. You better call in at about eight anyway. In case I have something for you. Goodbye.'

Commander Moffet put the phone down and sank back in his chair. He sat for a moment deep in thought. He considered, in the way he might have considered buying an abstract painting, whether he was capable of disobeying an order. He flirted with the idea but in the end rejected it utterly. He might secretly wish that Plover had not told him Schulz's plans, but now that he knew, nothing could stop him passing the information up the line. In a way, he told himself with a slight feeling of regret, it was a relief not to have the responsibility for making the decision.

He picked up one of the ordinary black telephones on his desk and asked to be connected with the Deputy Assistant Commissioner.

The intelligence that an attempt was to be made on the life of President Amin at or during the Queen's Birthday Parade was duly communicated by the Head of Special Branch to the Commissioner of the Metropolitan Police and the Permanent Under-Secretary at the Home Office, where the matter was given top priority. After ministerial discussion the decision to warn Amin about the attempt and advise him against attending the Parade on Saturday came from the Prime Minister himself. By six o'clock an appointment had been arranged for the Home Secretary, accompanied by the Commissioner, to see the President in his suite at the Inn on the Park. As senior officer in charge of security for the Commonwealth Conference, Commander Moffet was also asked to be in attendance.

They arrived at the hotel at four minutes to seven and were met at the door by two of the President's aides, who accompanied them in the lift up to the penthouse suite, where they were ushered in and offered cocktails by a glamorous hostess who introduced herself as 'H.E.'s personal assistant.' They were then kept waiting for ten minutes. Just as Commander Moffet was beginning to wish that he'd accepted a drink after all and the Home Secretary, growing increasingly impatient, was on the point of asking one of the aides for some explanation, the President walked in unexpectedly from the corridor wearing a striped silk dressing gown with Uganda's crest emblazoned on the back.

'I apologise for the delay, gentlemen, but I was held up. An unavoidable circumstance!" He smiled gravely and shook hands with each of them in turn. 'I hope my attendants have given you good entertainments. Please make yourselves comfortable.' He waved the Minister and the two policemen on to a sofa and made a sign to the girl and the aides who promptly withdrew. As soon as they had left the room, he sat down in an armchair opposite the British delegation and lay back, one arm sprawling. He smiled engagingly. 'I am interested to hear from you, Mr. Rees, on this matter of grave importance concerning my personal securities.'

The Home Secretary cleared his throat and in a few brief sentences explained the situation, offering the Government's apologies, but suggesting firmly that the President would be well advised to avoid the risk attached to his coming to tomorrow's ceremony. While he spoke Bill Moffet kept a close watch on the President's face and found there some confirmation of the theories he had formed of the man's character. No question of clinical madness or syphilitic decay. He saw in the dark brooding eyes and uneasy frown the suspicious nature of a peasant corrupted by absolute power, a black Stalin, whose obsession with his own survival had turned him, through the labyrinth of paranoia, into a monster. And yet the man had undeniable charm and a sort of genius for setting protocol on its head and pointing out all that was ridiculous about world politics, the law and national government – usually to his own advantage. He looked in his face for signs of fear, but if it was there nothing showed. When Mr. Rees had finished, the President roared with laughter and clapped his hands together.

'Mr. Home Secretary, there is no question I am attending the Queen's Jubilee Ceremony. This is one of the chief reasons why I have come here from Uganda. The Trooping Colour ceremony is famous to me and this entertainments was not available during my last visit. You must tell your police they are acting like womens, to pull their socks up pretty quick and dig out these C.I.A. agents and Zionist Israeli plotters who are bringing this dirty game against me.'

'But President, I must point out that the danger is real and considerable and that in the circumstances neither the Commissioner nor Commander Moffet feel able to vouch for your security.'

The President suddenly rose from his chair and walked over to the windows. Standing with his back to them he remained silent for an effective length of time. Then he said softly, 'Consider, please, very carefully: if something is made against me tomorrow at the ceremony and I am killed, who will be living in Uganda to vouch for the security of the 200 or so British nationals who are still there? I am responsible for their safety. You are responsible for mine. Do you understand my meaning?'

He swung round and with his back to the light looked at the three men on the sofa. They said nothing, but it was apparent to him that they understood his meaning all too well.

Schulz began packing the Weatherby into a green sporting hold-all a little larger than an airline bag. He had adapted the rifle to his needs: no longer recognisable as the beautifully made sporting gun it once was, it had been cut into three short segments that screwed together to make a different sort of weapon. The barrel and bolt body and been sawn off behind the trigger guard and the old stock removed: he had replaced it by an aluminium skeleton frame with a rubber shoulder grip. The barrel itself had been sawn in half and the last ten inches substituted with a thick tube silencer and a prong-type flash suppressor. The high gloss finish and tooled stock-wood, which characterised the Weatherby, had vanished under a coat of thick matt paint. The whole assembly, apart from the bolt housing, had been daubed in the greens, browns and greys of field camouflage.

The four-power telescopic sight permanently fitted to the bolt body in the middle section of the rifle had to be handled with care: the slightest knock could put the sighting out of alignment. Schulz swathed it in mutton cloth before laying it between the layers of clothing that lined the bottom of the green hold-all. He then took from his pocket the sheet metal box magazine and a carton of Weatherby proprictory ·460 Magnums. He removed three from the greased paper wrapping and examined each of them in turn. It gave him a peculiar pleasure to consider what were undoubtedly the most powerful sporting cartridges in the world and he handled them as if they were objects of great value. The tip of each cartridge had been removed and a cross filed into the soft glittering lead of the nose. At a range of up to 400 yards they would knock a hole as big as a saucer in the side of an elephant. Schulz clipped the three slugs into the magazine – it was as many as it would hold, but he had no intention of using more than one – and put it back in his trouser pocket. Then he knelt down and zipped up the hold-all.

Everything was in order. He looked at his watch. It gave 7.45. Plenty of time. He took a long swig of cognac from the half bottle that lay on the camp bed, then slipped it into the pocket of his leather coat. He stood up and adjusted his shoulder holster for comfort and took several deep breaths. First he would have a good dinner at a restaurant and then perhaps go and see a movie. After that he would make his decision.

'Dead on time for once, Plover. I just got back from an educating cocktail with the fat man. The show is over. We're going to bring you all in . . .'

'Bolting the stable door.'

'Now from what we know of Schulz, there may be some shooting. I want the layout . . .'

'You're too late. Schulz went out a quarter of an hour ago. The others have gone too. I wasn't there. Trying to get a call through. Look, it's difficult to know what's happening. Nobody said a thing.

'Is he coming back?'

'The room's empty. The gun sacks have gone. And the Mercedes. The others have left all their stuff.'

'Right, well stay there and wait. We'll sent a car round to keep an eye on the front. If no-one's back by midnight, we'll come in and take a sniff round.'

'They may have gone to his place in Willesden or to one of the others.'

'We'll check them all.'

'Christ, what a mess. I'm sorry, chief.'

'Not your fault, Plover.'

# SIX

At 11.15 Schulz came out of the Eros cinema on Piccadilly Circus and turned into Lower Regent Street. He stopped for a moment by the entrance to the Underground and looked quickly around at the Friday night crowds, a maelstrom of pale, neon-stained faces. He shuddered and an expression of disgust which took in the entire human species crossed his sensitive features; then he ran down the steps into the station. Across the road by the Criterion entrance a black man in a check sports coat followed his example.

A few minutes later Schulz reappeared carrying the green hold-all and set off down Piccadilly, walking slowly, trying to decide whether to go through with it for the extra five thousand or not. It should have been simple. A question of weighing the rewards against the risk involved. But somehow that wasn't quite it. Things went deeper than that with him; they always had done. He hadn't fought in three wars and risked his life God knows how many times just for money. There was more at stake. Steiner used to call it personal honour: it had been his only allegiance. But Schulz had other, more complicated ideas. His was a warped notion of glory. Perhaps his memories of the purges at Mutukula had scarred him too deeply, or he had been too long alone sitting at his window overlooking Gladstone Park, but he suffered from a compulsion to destroy. It was the idea of not completing something he had brought so far, so close to perfection, which held and fascinated him. The thrill of holding back, pulling out, waiting – a private negative charge that was high in sexual content. As he turned down into St. James's, Schulz came to his decision and the sudden release from the anxiety of failing filled him with exultation. He laughed aloud and tears welled in his dull grey eyes.

A shadow fell in behind him, but he was too absorbed with his thoughts to notice. He had to make one last trip to the scene of his 'crime.' He smiled at the idea and stopping on the edge of the Mall, already decked out with flags for tomorrow's ceremony, he looked up and down the long broad sweep of road for any sign of police activity. Apart from a couple of bobbies outside St. James's Palace, all was clear. He crossed the Mall and walked along under the shadow of the park trees as the sound of brass and the thump of drums inside his head trained his feet into a sort of march. He would come and watch. That would be the final irony. The others would be waiting for it to happen and all the time he would be out there relaxing and enjoying the parade.

Schulz entered the park and, keeping to the trees, moved carefully down through the dark and silent greenery towards the pond. He had come this route so many times over the past month he could do it with his eyes closed. The park was never patrolled after midnight. Sometimes a policeman walked through, but you could hear them coming a mile away and the park attendants were as regular as clockwork in their habits. Once or twice he'd come across down-and-outs sleeping under the trees; and in the last couple of weeks, with the warmer weather, couples came in for sex, but they never stayed long. He'd been lucky: it had all been so easy.

He crossed the grass and walked down the little slope that led on to Horse Guards. As he drew level with a stand of beech trees, he heard a twig snap close behind him. He swung round. An arm encircled his neck. A hand was clamped over his mouth. He felt the knife at his throat and then came a whisper in his ear. 'Hullo, Schulz. No cause for alarm. I'm just here to keep you company. This could be a long night spent on your own.'

He recognised the voice. 'Osaya. What the hell are you doing here?' he whispered angrily. 'Do you want to mess everything up? Clear off, you stupid bastard. And let me get on with it.'

The grip tightened on his throat. 'Careful Mr. Schulz, remember I never had much time for you. But the friends want me to make sure you don't change your mind at the last moment. So I'll be staying with you from now until the time you pull that trigger. You got it?'

'Let go so I can talk.'

Osaya eased the pressure on his neck and, keeping the

knife to his throat, slowly turned his man around until he was facing him. Then he slipped his hand inside the leather coat and drew out Schulz's hand gun. "So you can talk now.'

'You're mad,' Schulz hissed through the dark. 'You're going to spoil all my arrangements. There is no room for two on this job.'

'It will be less comfortable, but there is room. I checked.'

'What do you mean?' he gasped.

'You didn't think I was going to let you go ahead without knowing how? I followed you here before.' Osaya laughed softly. 'I saw you empty the sacks of earth into the lake.'

Schulz gave a bitter sigh. 'Do the others know?'

'I told Michael I would stay with you to the end, but I never mentioned your hiding place.'

'Why not?'

'The fewer people know a thing the better.'

Schulz sneered. 'You've got a nerve and all that talk about throwing grenades. Did you tell your girl Sally?'

'Not even her.'

Schulz considered alternatives. He felt a strong urge to run, but the knife was pricking at his throat. He was trapped. The sudden realisation reduced all his evasions to nothing. He would have to go through with it. He felt almost relieved. 'All right, if I have no choice,' he whispered, already resigned to his fate, 'but you will make it more difficult. The responsibility is yours.'

'We are too long standing here. You go ahead and I come behind you.'

Schulz turned and began to walk. They came out on to the great empty Parade of Horse Guards and, passing behind the monument, followed the path round by the bank of flowers, where it curves in to join the approach road to the H.Q. of the Royal Parks Constabulary. The place was in darkness and as quiet as a cemetery. Schulz swung the green hold-all up on to the mound close to the wattle fence and climbed up behind it, signalling Osaya to follow. There was a strip of hardened earth along the bottom of the fence, which he always used to avoid leaving footprints. But there had been no rain for a couple of weeks and the precaution was scarcely necessary. Getting down on hands and knees he crawled under the bushes at the top of the mound just in front of the fence and, removing his marker, a £5 note folded lengthways and stuck into the earth, he prepared to open up the dug-out.

Unzipping the hold-all he produced two long screw-drivers with sharpened points, which he pushed down into the earth in front of him. When they met with resistance, he gave each in turn a couple of hard shoves until they were stuck fast. Pulling on them together, he slowly raised the edge of the trap door until he could get a hand underneath. The smell of damp earth was suddenly overpowering. Twisting out the screwdrivers, he cleaned them on the sleeve of his coat and put them back in the hold-all; then he lifted the earth-covered hatch with both hands and carefully moved it back on to the ground beside the darker shadow of the dug-out.

Schulz reached up inside the bush and picked a good handful of leaves which he shoved inside his coat pocket. Then he climbed down into the hole, taking care to disturb the crumbling soil as little as possible. He whispered to Osaya and the African handed down the hold-all and joined him in the pit.

The crystal numerals of Schulz's watch glowed red in the dark. It was fifteen minutes after midnight.

Inspector Loveridge stood in the middle of the room and looked round the four empty walls. One of his men came in behind him and began to move about in a purposeful way, but he signalled him to leave. He walked over to the fire-place and, carefully drawing up the creases of his twill trousers, lowered himself on to his hunkers. There was nothing in the grate but dust and a piece of brown netting, which looked as if it had been cut out from a larger section. It was newer than the dust, but that was about all that could be said for it. He dropped it into an envelope and rose to his feet. There were the emptyings of ashtrays in the waste-paper basket and a couple of half-full mugs of cold coffee lying around; otherwise the cupboard was about as bare as it could be. Loveridge sniffed twice. He recognised paint, the smell of paint, but the other aroma was more delicate, difficult . . .

He pushed back his trilby – he was always forgetting to take it off on entering premises – and drew a tentative hand across his chin testing for stubble. He was tired and he'd been out of luck for too long.

He sniffed again. Johnson's Baby Powder – that was it. If he looked around the floor he'd probably find traces. Schulz didn't have women or any visitors, so that meant . . . He gave up the line of thought in disgust.

There would be 12,000 people watching the parade tomorrow from the stands and God knows how many more hiving around the park end. It would be impossible to check them all. If Schulz had a ticket to the ceremony there might be a fair chance of picking him up. But loose among the crowd, he was going to be hard to catch. A window on to the parade ground – the search would start tomorrow morning early. That was no longer in his hands. The Foreign Office was a possibility. Inspector Loveridge gave a weary sigh. With the lives of 200-odd Britons at stake, it had to be a Kraut, didn't it, with his bloody finger on the trigger? He looked at his watch. In less than twelve hours' time the man would be making his play.

'It was a small but well-used track,' the whisper came out of the darkness, 'leading off into the jungle. So we followed it up. I sent one of my black sergeants and a bunch of scouts a few hundred yards out in front. Pretty soon one of them comes running back all excited and says they've found an underground armour dump. It's got a makeshift door on it – a bit like this one here – but they'd seen the boxes inside by using a torch to peer through a crack.

'While the scout was talking, suddenly there was this tremendous explosion which shook the ground under our feet and knocked us flat. We got up and ran forward. There was a huge smoking crater in the ground made by the blast. All the surrounding trees had been stripped white – no leaves, no branches, no bark, nothing. The sergeant and his scouts were gone, literally blown to pieces. We picked up some remains further off. Hands, bits of flesh, twisted legs: I found a rib cage and a wrist with a tattoo marking that I recognised. It was a booby trap, of course, left by the rebels . . .'

Schulz suddenly stopped talking and listened. Nothing stirred. It was one of the advantages of their position – being so close to the road and sitting on top of the Park's Police H.Q., they could hear anybody approaching from either side. It meant they would be able to leave the lid off at least until dawn. The dug-out was well hidden by the bushes: no danger of being seen, except from the front, and that was only a few square inches among the leaves. When the time came to batten down he would fix up the air tube. He had left a hole in the wooden hatch and a small pipe ran up through the earth covering. Now there were two of them it would be essential if they were to avoid suffocating. It was a good thing too he had made the dug-out larger than strictly necessary. Even so, assembly was going to be difficult and . . . damn the black bastard's eyes . . . but if it hadn't been for him, he realised shamefully, he wouldn't be here at all.

'Why do you tell me such stories?' Osaya asked softly. He was squatting down on the floor of the pit, his face a few inches from Schulz's. 'I was a soldier too. I know these things.'

'That was the Biafra campaign.'

'Was it? I wonder sometimes, Schulz. Some of your stories sound so familiar. You sure you never set foot in Uganda?'

'Quite sure.'

'Remember I told you about my father, who was killed at Mutukula when Amin purged the Langi and Acholi. Well, I was put into Makindye prison soon afterwards and I was in a cell there with a man who survived that massacre. He was raving a bit by then, but he told me there was a white man in charge of the operation . . ."

'Why are you telling me this?' Schulz's voice hovered in his throat.

'I think *you* are trying to tell me something. Were you ever with the Anyana in the Sudan?'

'No I . . .' he hesitated, wondering if Michael could have told him.

'But Rolf Steiner was.'

'Maybe, I don't know. I didn't see him again after Onitsha.'

'You're lying, Schulz. I believe you were there in Sudan. Perhaps you came to Uganda too. See all your lies. Perhaps you were in prison and Amin released you for work in the army. Why did you think none of us would know this is your history? The things you did at Mutukula cannot be forgotten.'

There was a pause, then Schulz said, 'I never heard of that name, You've got the wrong man. There were plenty of whites in Uganda at that time, but I was never there. I give you my word.'

'It's nearly daylight.' Osaya changed the subject.

'You are right,' Schulz whispered gratefully, 'It's time to batten down. We have to manoeuvre carefully so as not to disturb the outside. Here, come on, you give me a hand.'

'What happens if they use dogs to search the bushes?'

'They are bound to do so and what's more, they have my scent. But I have taken precautions. All my clothes and shoes are impregnated with a special mustard preparation used by the German Pfadfinders, which has a numbing effect on the dog's nose and confuses the scent. I have been using it around this whole area on the bushes, the grass, everywhere for days.' Schulz laughed softly. 'I have also laid some false trails with lions' urine courtesy of London Zoo. That was a trick I learnt out in Africa. It drives them mad. You see, I have thought of everything.'

'What about my scent?'

'They won't be looking for you – not here.'

They lifted the hatch over their heads. The thickness of the earth covering was five inches, held in place by a strip of wire mesh around the edges. It was heavy and had to be lowered slowly to make sure of a right fit. When it was down, Schulz flashed a pencil torch to check the inside seam. He then fixed up the air tube. They readjusted their positions and settled down to wait.

With even less room than before, they were forced into an almost unbearable proximity. The sickly scent of baby powder rose in Osaya's nostrils. It was like the sweet fetid smell of death. He thought of how his father must have felt, thrown into a pit like this with maybe twenty or thirty others, all crammed together, waiting for the charges to be dropped in on top of them.

He wanted to tell him now, so he could spend the few hours he had left knowing that he was never going to climb out of this hole. But it might spoil his nerve. He would get his revenge tomorrow. But only after Schulz had served his purpose.

## SEVEN

*Saturday, 11th June*
It was a perfect morning. The sun shone from a cloudless sky and warmed the long empty swathe of pink road which the Mall cut through the vivid green avenue of trees. A light breeze stirred the glistening foliage; flags, bright daubs of colour, fluttered from white poles at regular intervals along the way; and faint ripples disturbed the black bearskins of the motionless guardsmen who lined both kerbs. Behind the twin rows of navy blue, scarlet and white the banks of spectators, half hidden by the overhanging trees, reached from the Queen Victoria Monument to Admiralty Arch and along the short slip road that turns down into Horse Guards, where more than 12,000 people sat in tiered stands along three sides of the rectangular parade ground – all of them waiting for the Queen. It was 10.30.

On the Parade two long ranks of guardsmen stood in an L-shaped formation fronting the spectators on the north side, below the mildew-green roofs and red brick façade of the Admiralty, and to the west, the open flank, where St. James's Park completes the fourth side of the rectangle. The 360-strong Massed Bands of the Household Brigade were formed up under the south stands in front of the group of buildings which include the Treasury, the Scottish Office and behind them, across Downing Street, the Foreign Office. The Queen, when she arrived, would take up her position in front of the Archway on the east side of the parade ground under the putty-grey walls of Horse Guards itself. It was here that the guests of honour were mostly seated; a special stand had been reserved for the Commonwealth Heads of State by the north-east corner.

In the buildings surrounding the Parade, spectators were gathered at every vantage point, but despite the warm weather all windows overlooking the square were kept closed by order of the police. Every room in every building had been checked and double checked since dawn. On the roofs, security men scanned the terraces through binoculars and police snipers in shirt sleeves lay out along the parapets barely hidden from sight. Uniformed and plain clothes police moved through the crowds along the Mall and in the park, checking faces against Schulz's photofit; asking anyone who had climbed up a tree or lamp post for a better view to come down; examining suspicious-looking cases and packages on the pretext of a bomb scare.

But the numbers involved made it a hopeless task; against the relentless advance of the clock the security forces fought a losing battle. By 10.45, as the distant clatter of hooves on Constitution Hill announced the arrival of the Sovereign's Escort of the Household Cavalry at the gates of Buckingham Palace, the search for Dieter Schulz and his fellow conspirators had drawn a blank.

The idea that he'd missed something at the flat in Drayton Gardens had been nagging at Inspector Loveridge since early morning. He'd come away last night convinced that he'd turned up every possible trace of Schulz's short stay in that room. If it had amounted to next to nothing, he hadn't needed Bill Moffet to point it out to him, but there was something there, he knew it, and as the precious hours and minutes evaporated in the slow routine procedures of the search, his anxiety grew into a conviction. With less than a quarter of an hour to go before the Queen arrived on the parade ground, he made the decision to disobey orders and go back to the flat, taking the girl with him.

With the help of the siren and some skilful driving by the sergeant, they arrived in Drayton Gardens at two minutes after eleven. The girl let him in with her keys and they went straight to Schulz's room. It was slightly improved by daylight, but nothing could relieve the drab dankness of those peeling walls. The place needed doing up, but that was it – the smell of paint.

'Did Schulz ever lend a hand with the decorating?'

'No. Anyway that was just a pretext for this place. It never got further than the front room.'

'But I can smell paint in here.' Loveridge sniffed. 'It was

here last night and it's here now.'

'Wait a second,' the girl frowned, 'he did borrow a paint-brush one evening. He didn't say what for . . .'

'If he put it back, it would be in the sitting room with the other stuff. Right?' Inspector Loveridge was already on his way out of the door. 'Would you remember which brush it was?'

'Small, a half inch at the most, for doing window frames and that sort of thing.' she called after his disappearing back. She followed him along the passage to the front of the flat, running to keep up, her shoes clicking across the dusty parquet.

Loveridge was kneeling down behind the sofa examining a tray of paint pots, rollers, brushes and other decorating paraphernalia. He gave a sigh of satisfaction and pulled out a slim brush from a jar of turps. He held it up to the girl.

'Is this it? Green was the last colour.'

'It looks like it. I think there was only one that size. But he must have used his own paint. I never bought any green . . .'

'Or field grey, or khaki brown, I'll wager; but the cans are here. Recognise any of these? Loveridge, by now thoroughly excited, pushed forward the paint tins.

'No, I don't. Nor do I see the significance.'

'Camouflage. That's what . . . and, of course, it's so obvious. A man of his training. That piece of netting I found last night, it's for sticking leaves and stuff in. What a bloody idiot I've been.'

The double line of guardsmen drawn up across the west side of the Parade, opposite the Archway, had parted to allow the passage of the Royal Family's carriages from the Mall and then swung back to re-form their original line. At four minutes to eleven they repeated the first part of the manoeuvre to await the arrival of the Queen and her escort.

The perfectly symmetrical cavalry formation had reached the top of the Mall, a column of black horses mounted by troopers, whose helmets, cuirasses and swords rising vertically from white gauntlets and glittering in the sun, all jingled and clinked at every clattering step their mounts took. The First and Second Divisions, accompanied by the Mounted Band caparisoned in gold cloth, which rode in front of the Sovereign, now breached the line of scarlet-tunicked guardsmen and entered the parade ground. At the moment when the Queen reached the north-west corner of Horse Guards, she split off from her escort and rode slowly on a diagonal course across the square towards the Archway, a solitary rider.

Behind her the mounted escort were forming up opposite the foot guards on the park side of the parade ground, the end trooper wheeling his horse into position as the clock in Horse Guards tower began to strike eleven and the Queen turned under the Archway to face the brilliant assembly. As the last chime rang out over the silent parade, the Massed Bands struck up the national anthem.

In pitch darkness Schulz reached inside his coat pocket and felt for the hairnet. He drew it out and carefully spread it on his knees. The slight but unaccustomed movement sent lancings of pain through his cramped limbs. From the other pocket he produced the leaves and twigs he had taken from the bushes above the dug-out and began to twist them into the mesh of the net. When he had finished he pulled it over his head and stretched the sides down until they covered his ears. He could feel the twigs prickling his scalp and the bare skin of his neck. He adjusted the leaves in front until they formed a low fringe across his eyebrows.

Osaya was sucking noisily at the air tube. Schulz reached out and touched the African's face. It was wet with perspiration. 'Move back,' he whispered close to his ear. Osaya pressed himself against the wall of the dug-out as Schulz pulled up the hold-all from under their intertwined legs. First putting on a pair of green, soft leather ladies' gloves, he unzipped the bag and took out the three sections of the rifle. Placing the skeleton butt between his knees on the floor of the pit, he unwound the mutton cloth swaddling from the barrel, bolt body and fitted scope and screwed it on to the stock. Then he threaded on the silencer and flash suppressor, which brought the overall length of the Weatherby up to 45 inches, leaving 4 inches to spare under the wooden trap door. Keeping the rifle upright between his knees, Schulz tightened the joints until the leather of his gloves squeaked. From his trouser pocket, which was more difficult to get at, he produced the magazine and gently pushed it up into the magazine port until it locked with a faint click. All moving parts of the rifle had been heavily greased to reduce noise. Drawing back the bolt he eased a cartridge forward into the chamber – stopping at this point to check with his pencil torch that the slug was properly aligned – then pushed it home.

The music from the parade ground died. Schulz looked at his watch. It was 11.05. The Queen would be beginning her inspection, moving along the two front rows of the L-shaped formation, then down the back, passing her Cavalry Escort and returning to the Archway by 11.15, where she would remain for the rest of the ceremony. Next the Massed Bands would perform, the guardsmen would receive the Colour, the Colour Escort would parade and at 11.30 the trooping would finally begin. Schulz had studied the programme till he knew each manoeuvre by heart. The timing would be split-second – to be relied on absolutely. At 11.35 the Colour would go before the Queen lowered in salute, but as it passed the tiered stands the spectators, bound by tradition, would all have to rise to their feet . . .

Earlier Schulz had made a single reconnaissance. He had never doubted that once the man had entered the country he would attend this ceremony, but he had to see exactly where he was sitting. Easing up the lid of the trap door on his shoulders and peering out from the inside of the bush through the small bright gap framed by dark leaves, he had looked across the parade ground to the stands in the north-east corner occupied by the Commonwealth V.I.P.s. The massive bulk of President Amin, partly hidden from view by the bearskins of the foot guards, eight yards from where Schulz was hidden, was unmistakable. A smile of satisfaction had spread his lips: the target was in position.

Inspector Loveridge had radioed from his car on the way back to Horse Guards. Arriving with a squeal of tyre rubber at the corner of Queen Street and Birdcage Walk, he saw with relief that his instructions were already being carried out. The trees, bushes, grass verges and flower beds along the whole length of the east side of St. James's Park were being scoured by uniformed police. It was ground that had been covered twice before that morning, but now the odds had been reduced. The seated spectators, crowds and buildings could be ignored and the search concentrated on natural terrain. An obvious choice was the trees, but few with any sort of view over the parade ground could have concealed a man. Officers with binoculars stood beneath the tallest beeches and limes and gazed up into the June-green foliage, watched in their turn by curious bystanders, whose attention had been diverted from the ceremony by this new surge of police activity.

The clock in the tower above the Archway struck 11.30 as Loveridge, followed by the girl and a uniformed sergeant, ran across the edge of the park into Horse Guards and pushed their way through the throng held back by the thin line of guardsmen. Heading for the Monument directly opposite the Archway at the centre of the west side of the parade ground, Loveridge's only thought was that they were not yet too late.

The Massed Bands of the Household Brigade, wheeling and pivoting upon themselves, thumped out 'Hearts of Oak' as the foot guards formed into eight separate phalanxes and with the Colour Escort at their head marched in slow time up the south side of the Parade. As they passed before them, the seated spectators rose from their benches and stood silently as a mark of solemn respect. It was the arcane moment of the ceremony and the crowd seemed to share some strong emotion brought on by the impressive dignity of the occasion. At the Treasury corner the Guards turned and came slowly – a pause before each step – along the east side of the square towards the Queen, who sat like an equestrian statue in front of the Archway. Beyond her in the north-east corner the Commonwealth Heads of State craned their necks to watch the approaching Colour, eagerly waiting their turn to do as tradition demanded.

At precisely 11.33 Dieter Schulz placed his head and shoulders under the forward part of the hatch and slowly pushed up until the crack in front of him that let in light, music and air was wide enough to see out. The tunnel he had made through the middle of the bush allowed only a narrow perspective, limited on the right to a section of the Guards Monument barely 20 feet away with the names and dates of campaigns from the Great War clearly visible, but giving a longer view across the centre of the parade ground. Immediately in front of him he could see the heads of the crowd and beyond them the line of bearskins.

The elevation of the top of the mound above the level of the parade ground was an inch or two over seven feet. When he came to make the hit, his elbows over ground would give him another foot and a half in height. By then, across the other side of the Parade, 340 paced yards away, the target would have flipped up into full view allowing him a clear shot. There were two minutes to go. Schulz began to nose the barrel of the rifle out through the opening in the trap door. Suddenly he felt the ground shudder close behind his head. After a crash of cymbals from the Massed Bands he heard distinctly the sound of rustling leaves.

Quickly he pulled the rifle back and closed the hatch. He gripped Osaya's arm and neither man stirred a muscle as they listened with hearts thumping and sweat pricking at their eyes to the movements overhead. Somebody had crawled under the bush – there was a scuffling sound immediately above them – but then they heard a muffled voice say 'Over here,' and the heavy tread moved away along the top of the mound. Schulz wiped his face and looked at his watch. 11.34. Gritting his teeth he counted 30 seconds, then pushed up the hatch and shoved the rifle through, bringing up his elbows on to the earth lip of the dug-out. He raised the Weatherby and, closing one eye, sighted down the scope at the stands in the far corner of the Parade.

Straining his ears for the possible return of the footsteps, Osaya looked out over the mercenary's shoulder at the backs of the spectators immediately below them. As he kept watch, a minor disturbance in the crowd to the left of the Monument drew his attention. A moment later he saw a small, thin-faced man in a brown hat hurry across his limited field of vision. He was closely followed by a uniformed policeman and a girl with dark hair wearing a raincoat. He only caught a glimpse of her face, but he needed no more than that to recognise Superman's girl-friend: it was Sally Temple Owen.

More surprised than angry, Osaya gave no time to the thought that she had betrayed him. He saw her now only as an immediate threat to the success of their operation. Schulz, with one eye to the scope and the other closed, had seen nothing. He considered whether or not to warn him, but decided against it. By now the Guards had reached the north-east corner of the Parade and the Commonwealth leaders were getting to their feet. Osaya drew his knife.

Through the sights of the Weatherby, Schulz watched with intense emotion as President Amin rose to his full height. The Field Marshal stood proudly to attention as the Colour Escort passed below him. The hairline cross of the sights wavered, then came to rest on the massive chest and centred on the flamboyant rows of medals. The index finger on Schulz's right hand tightened on the single-pull trigger. Then the sights became blurred. Schulz let go his breath with a soft curse and looked over the top of the scope. A child's head had bobbed up in the gap. Sitting on the shoulders of a man, her blonde curls had come directly in line with his view of the target. Schulz put his eye back to the sights and waited.

Less than four yards away in the approach road to the H.Q. of the Parks Police, Loveridge fumed with indecision. On an impulse he climbed up on to the mound. Standing next to the bush that concealed the dug-out, he looked behind the wattle fence where the park attendants kept a small vegetable garden and then gazed up hopelessly into the high branches of the beech tree overhead. It occurred to him that he might have been wrong about the camouflage after all. His eyes came down to the level of the bushes, then moved slowly across the parade ground to the stands. There he was, the big black bastard. How could anyone miss? The President was saluting the Colour. Jesus Christ. Loveridge looked away. Perhaps Schulz was not even here. They only had the word of the girl. He looked down at his feet. A leaf curled under his shoe. And Special

Branch were always getting it wrong . . . He moved his foot. The stem of the leaf was torn.

Loveridge drew up the creases of his twill trousers and knelt down beside the bush. He picked up the leaf, rubbed it between his fingers and raised it to his nostrils. It gave off a pugent smell of chemicals. He looked more closely at the bush. In several places twig ends showed white, where they had been broken off – recently. He put a hand inside the bush and parted the branches, peering into the densest part of the thicket, hardly noticing the unnatural angle of the ground formed by the raised hatch. Then he saw the long green snout of the Weatherby.

The child's head moved a fraction. For a second he had a clear view of the target. Schulz squeezed off. In that same instant Loveridge threw himself into the bush and came down with all his weight on top of the hatch. The rifle was knocked from the mercenary's grasp. Schulz just had time to know that he'd missed, before failure was rewarded by Osaya's knife, which came up under his ribs and struck deep into his heart.

Below the Commonweath stand a Guardsman fell forward on to his face. The fourth casualty of the day. The reminder went down the line, 'Wiggle your toes and flex your knees.' It was assumed he had fainted and the man was left lying in the hot sun with a hole the size of a saucer in the front of his scarlet tunic. Then the blood began to flow.

# EIGHT

'Incidentally, where did you spend last night?' Commander Moffet looked up at them from the desk. 'Purely out of interest.' He began preening his facial hair with a pencil.

'We parked the Mercedes, I don't know, somewhere along . . .'

'*I* parked it,' Ruth interrupted him. '*I'm* the driver.' Her eyes sparked.

'Good for you,' Moffet said laconically. 'And neither of

you had any idea how Schulz was going to make the attempt? So even if we had picked you up earlier, we'd have been none the wiser . . . What did Osaya have against the mercenary?'

Michael shrugged his shoulders. 'Perhaps he tried to escape. I told him to follow and keep watch. We thought Schulz was going to let us down. Osaya never had much time for him anyway.'

'Schulz is no great loss, but I'm afraid your friend will have to stand trial for murder. And face conspiracy charges as well,' Moffet looked grave. 'The question is, what do we do with you two? The evidence against you is rather more than damning.'

'Because of that white bitch of Osaya's,' Ruth snorted indignantly, 'I always knew she was nothing but . . .'

"You're talking about one of my best officers,' Moffet smiled, 'Plover, I mean Sally, was only there to keep an eye on you, but I'm afraid things got too involved. You see, basically there was little objection to your removing Amin. As long as no question arose of the British Government being involved, we were prepared to turn a blind eye. But a decision was made high up to warn him about Schulz's attempt at the Trooping. That's when he caught us napping, I'm afraid. It was like this. If we let something happen to him – and I think he suspected we knew what was going on – what would happen to the 200 British nationals living in Uganda? His usual game of threatening a group of foreigners, but as always damn difficult to tell whether he's bluffing.'

"You mean, Amin said that he's made arrangements for something bad to happen to those people if he's killed?' Michael frowned.

'Not in so many words, but he implied as much.'

'He's not bluffing, let me tell you.'

'That's rather the impression we've been getting from reports out of Nairobi and the French Embassy in Kampala.'

'We were nearly successful,' Ruth said defiantly.

'But you understand why we had to intervene?'

Michael nodded.

'However, there is still something that could be done – '

Moffet paused ' – which might serve your purpose as well as ours. It's a little delicate, of course, but we should be able to come to some arrangement.'

'To kill Amin?' Michael sounded hopeful.

'No, I'm afraid that's out of the question now. At least on British soil. This is more a matter of causing him . . . embarrassment.'

'He's not easily embarrassed.' Michael did not try to hide his disappointment. 'And what sort of retribution is that for a man like him?'

'Well, I don't know if you are aware of it, but for the duration of his stay in Britain Amin left Uganda and the Armed Forces in charge of General Kitembe – not a man he trusts. There's been the usual purge of the Cabinet since his departure – no doubt organised beforehand – but Kitembe is too popular with the Army to risk eliminating so casually. Which is all the more reason for Amin not to trust him.'

'He doesn't trust anybody.'

'But in Kitembe's case he's taken certain rather unusual precautions. He's brought with him from Uganda, as part of his entourage, two of the General's children – hostages, if you like, to ensure his good behaviour.'

'I'm not sure I understand . . .' Michael fidgeted with his spectacles.

'What I am suggesting – and believe me, I don't enjoy suggesting it – is that if something should happen to those two children, it might go badly for Amin on his return to Uganda.'

'You mean if the blame should fall on his head?'

'Exactly.' Moffet looked down at his hands. 'I'm going to be quite frank with you. This is not at all the sort of thing that we go in for in this country, but in the circumstances . . . Of course, you'd be acting entirely on your own.'

'You want us to kill those children?' Michael stared in disbelief at the solid, reassuring figure of the policeman.

'We would take care of the rest – making it look like Amin's work – and then I'm sure we would be able to come to some arrangement over the conspiracy charges.'

'You try to blackmail us.' Michael jumped up angrily. 'I won't stoop to such a foul thing. Killing Amin, yes, God has given us that right. But who would raise his hand against . . .'

'Sit down, man, and consider carefully.' Moffet waved him back into his chair. 'To remove Amin from the seat of power, that is your object – not to kill him: if you succeed he will be as good as dead anyway. You sacrifice the two children, but think how many Ugandan lives will be saved.'

'So the end justifies the means? And you a representative of British law.'

'I don't like it any more than you do, but that's the way things stand.' Moffet's little round eyes were set hard. 'Now let me have your answer. Time is short.'

"We'll do it," said Ruth, before Michael could reply. He turned and stared at her for a long moment, then looked back at the Commander and reluctantly nodded his head.

"Good. Now let's get down to business.' Moffet leaned forward rubbing his hands. 'Scotland. Your plane leaves in two hours' time. Plover will brief you on the way to the airport.'

# *Part Five*

# NEMESIS

## ONE

The Master of Ceremonies rose to his feet and, dusting the crumbs of a six-course dinner from the front of his kilt, threaded his way between the tables towards the stage. Coffee and liqueurs were now being served in the Glen Devon room and the hum of multi-lingual conversation had risen to a level of conviviality that swamped the background efforts of the five-piece orchestra. But as the kilted M.C. reached the microphone and, with a polite cough that reverberated through the amplifiers, began his announcement, the banqueters quietened down. It was the moment they had all been waiting for – the high spot of the evening. The music had died, but somewhere in the distance the hesitant groans and skirls of pipers tuning up drifted along the labyrinthine corridors of Gleneagles and the air was filled with Highland promise.

Welcoming the Commonwealth Heads of State to Scotland, the M.C. ran through a well-rehearsed speech that was rich in superlatives and expressions of international goodwill, ending up on a few safe jokes about the Scottish national character. Which led him easily into presenting the evening's entertainment – a display of Highland dancing interpreted by members of the Royal Perth Dance Academy. Only that morning on Horse Guards Parade, he reminded the delegates, they had witnessed the greatest English ceremonial; now they were in for something completely different, but equally magnificent . . . At that moment the doors of the Glen Devon burst open and four pipers, elbowing their bags for extra air to launch the tune, marched into the room playing "Scotland the Brave." Behind them came tripping eight girls and eight men wearing the Royal Stuart tartan, electric blue doublets and at their throats cheap lace jabots. The whole ensemble ground to a synchronised halt just below the stage, where a semicircle of floor had been cleared for action immediately in front of the banquet tables.

In the first row, not too far from the wall and a nearby exit (ensured therefore both of a good view of the dancing and an escape route in case of shooting), President Idi Amin of Uganda, draped from head to foot in tartan, velvet and lace, sat beaming at the pipers and dancers over a large tumbler of Drambuie. Beside him sat his aides and his "personal assistant," who was beautifully turned out in a long evening dress and turban of some blue and gold African material. Just as the display was about to begin she leant across and whispered something in his ear. For an answer he gave a curt nod. The girl got up and, leaving the table, made a quiet exit covered by the sudden explosion of obligatory yells as the first reel of the evening swirled into motion.

It was easy enough to lose one's way in the great hotel. From the Glen Devon, a large semi-circular function room with bow windows looking east towards the Ochil Hills, the President's personal assistant walked due west, which took her through the deserted golden ballroom and out again – after a rapid change of course – by the Gleneagles Post Office and Bank. She turned left and came back to Reception, where she was obliged to admit that she was lost and could not find her room. A bellboy was dispatched to show her the way and they set off together along interminable corridors, past the American Bar, Barony Lounge, shops, cinema, squash court and a billiards room, until they reached the South Wing. The bellboy pointed down the softly-lit passage and smiled obligingly, waiting only a second too long before wheeling smartly and returning unrewarded to his post.

Outside the door of room 234 the President's Personal

Assistant stood and listened for a moment, while she took her key from a slim evening bag. From next door came a low sound of men talking, but in 234 all was quiet. Inserting the key in the lock she turned it softly and opening the door with infinite care, entered on tiptoe.

The room was dark and stuffy. She stood in the vestibule and reached a hand along the wall, feeling for the handle of the bathroom door. Finding the switch she turned on the light in the bathroom, leaving the door ajar to give some illumination. Her long skirts rustling, she advanced into the middle of the room and peered down at the twin beds. The first was empty, but in the next bed there were two small dark heads on the pillow. With the covers thrown back Sarah and Nathan, the children of General Kitembe, lay in their pyjamas, arms and legs entwined, breathing with soft regularity, asleep. The President's assistant, coming closer, reached down to touch their foreheads. They were wet with perspiration. The room was unbearably hot. She pulled some of the covers back over them and walked across to the window. After a moment's hesitation she put her hand behind the curtains, undid the snib and lifted the sash a few inches.

As the floodlit roof of Gleneagles, with the thirty-six flags of the Commonwealth hugging their poles in the windless night, loomed above the tops of the Scots firs, Ruth began to slow down. They drove past the entrance to the hotel and Michael turned in his seat to look at the array of police motorcycles parked outside the lodge gates. Leaving the hotel on their left, they continued along the A873 in the direction of Crieff for half a mile or so, until Michael pointed out rather unnecessarily an enormous Dutch barn standing in a field behind a white farm gate. Ruth pulled into the side of the road and stopped the engine. She switched off the lights and they sat for a few moments getting used to the darkness. In the eastern sky across the golf courses and beyond the meadows of Strathearn there was still light above the Ochil Hills, but night was drawing in quickly. Ruth wound down her window. The air was cool and carried a scent of newly mown grass.

'Have you got the maps?' she asked without looking at him.

'I just want to have one more look before we go.' Michael produced a small torch which they had bought at the airport and began to study the map of the grounds and the floor plan of the hotel.

'Well, we have got here at least. The Queen's golf course is just over that wall and somewhere down there is the lake called . . . "Loch-An-Eerie," or however you pronounce it. So we might as well get into position. We can't sit here too long.'

Ruth didn't move. 'I still think we should go for Amin himself and forget the children.'

'But it was you who agreed to it.'

'Because it gave us this chance. Where would we be now, if we refused?'

Michael was silent. 'It would be impossible. Didn't they say he had bodyguards with him in his bedroom all the time? And here in the adjoining room.' He pointed down at the plans. 'It is going to be bad enough getting to the children . . . what if the security man forgets to leave the keys?'

'You are always making excuses,' Ruth said antagonistically, 'Why don't I do it? I could kill. I wouldn't lose my nerve . . .'

'Will you shut up?' Michael turned on her. 'Just shut up and listen to me. We have got two chances only. One is here tonight at the hotel and the other at Scone Airfield tomorrow morning when he goes to inspect the trainee pilots. Tonight is our best hope, by a long chalk; but if something goes wrong I want to be sure that one of us can take up that second opportunity – hopefully both of us. You have your instructions for tonight and you will obey them. Do you understand?'

Ruth took the key out of the ignition and, stuffing it into her pocket, angrily reached for the door handle. Michael caught her arm.

'Look, everything is going to be all right, darling. It has to be done. That is all there is to think of. I won't fail you and you will be waiting for me and it will be all right.'

Ruth sniffed and nodded her head, but said nothing in case her tears, hidden by the dark, should show in her voice.

They climbed out of the Hertz Corsair and left it without bothering to lock the doors. Looking up and down the empty road, Michael climbed up the wall and, giving Ruth a hand up, jumped down into the grounds of Gleneagles.

The Strathspey was brought to a neat conclusion and the dancers, bowing first to themselves and then to their audience, who clapped enthusiastically, picked up the crossed claymores from the floor and with the pipers at their head marched trippingly from the room. At once the M.C. was back on stage, waiting for the applause to die down, holding up his hands in smiling protest. He stepped up to the microphone. 'Thank you, Ladies and Gentlemen, thank you.' He coughed, a professional sound. 'You know, in Scotland we are very proud of our traditions, our dancing, music, whisky and what-have-you, as I am sure you all are in your own countries.' His faint Edinburgh accent became refined to a point of extinction. 'Most of our Scottish lore stems in point of fact from our wild and warlike past . . .' a pause '. . . when we fought mostly amongst ourselves, admittedly, but a great deal also against our neighbours, the English.' Laughter . . . 'However, we have all grown more civilised since then.' He cleared his throat to cover this slightly awkward choice of phrase and continued, 'Now, instead of war we have devolution.' He waited for more laughter, but it was a little slow in coming. 'But, of course, Scotland has all that lovely oil,' he added, 'and you know what they say about our being tight. If the English want to share it, they will have to pay – or fight for it!' He raised a clenched fist.

This time the audience laughed and clapped without restraint and the M.C. smiled happily, at the same time shaking his head from side to side as if to disclaim responsibility for the harmless but slightly risky jibe. Still smiling, he was about to continue his turn, when out of the corner of his eye, he noticed something which wiped the grin from his face. At one of the front row tables on the far side of the room an enormous black, tartan-clad figure had risen to his feet and, clapping loudly with his hands above his head, was bearing down on the stage with a purposeful look in his eye.

The audience fell silent as the Ugandan leader mounted

the steps and emerged suddenly from behind the curtains in a blaze of light. The kilted M.C., quite overshadowed by the vast tartan presence, was for the moment at a loss how to handle the situation. But he quickly recovered his aplomb. 'And now, Ladies and Gentlemen, a few words from President Idi Amin of Uganda, who has . . .'

A large black hand reached in front of him and collared the microphone. The M.C.'s voice dried up and, smiling bravely, he beat an embarrassed retreat, to take refuge with the band at the back of the stage.

'Hello, Ladies and Gentlemen, good evening.' The President spread his pink palms and inclined his head politely to the mortified gathering. 'I am taking this unusual step in speaking to you, because I have some important things to say. The Conference is not yet ended, and we are here for continued informal discussion, so please, I am making my position clear.

'The people of Scotland, we are all hearing, are sick and tired of being exploited by the English. This is true. Which is why the leaders of the Scottish Provincial Government have approached me to bring their case for total independence to the United Nations Committee on Decolonisation. Everyone knows that England is now bankrupt and are dealing systematically with headaches of tribalism. They are seriously plotting to exploit Scotland further, by grabbing out the money to be obtained from North Sea Oil. I am very happy Mr. . . . of Ceremonies –' He waved a hand towards the M.C. ' – is also pointing out that unless the Scots achieve their independence peacefully, they will take up arms and fight the English.

'But I must warn the Scottish Nationalists this is no joking matter for them. I am really very serious on what I am saying. We are living here near the home of Rob Roy, who was a brilliant revolutionary leader, like me, but the Scottish Nationalists' leaders are muddled thinkers and weak like womens. They have been brainwashed by the English and put in their pockets. This is why the revolutionary Scottish Provincial Government have asked me, General Amin, to be their leader. In fact many people in this country, I am also happy to tell you, regard me already as the King of Scotland. If the Scots want me to be their King,

I am ready.'

The President smiled broadly and drew a hand across his brow. His audience had not warmed to his impromptu speech and at the back of the Glen Devon room there were audible murmurings of protest and disapproval. Among the ranks of Perthshire notables, who had been invited to the banquet to lend tone to the proceedings, one or two old colonels and their wives had walked out, followed by some of the braver Commonwealth leaders. But the President was quite unperturbed.

'As you may have noticed I am wearing my own tartan. Actually I am calling this one "Black Watch".' He roared with laughter. Between a forest-green velvet smoking jacket, which spilled a profusion of lace from the cuffs and a pair of brogues with bright silver buckles, the President was wearing Campbell tartan trews. 'You see, I strongly believe in the Scottish peoples and their determination to win independence. The Scottish are among the bravest people I know . . . In fact, I am telling you this. I was promoted by Scottish officers from Lance-Corporal to Major during the British Colonial days.' At the back of the Glen Devon another colonel rose to his feet and made a hurried exit. 'In this way the Scots people have helped make me President of Uganda and one of the most brilliant and powerful figures in the world. This I want to make it absolutely clear: I am willing to help them now in their struggles against the Imperialists in Whitehall, who just this morning were trying once more to assassinate me . . .

'Miraculously, by God's will, I escaped.' The President held up his arms. 'And now I am inviting everyone tomorrow to Scone Airfield, where I am training beautiful Uganda girl pilots to fly aeroplanes, Russian MiG–21 jets, for suicide missions against South Africa and Rhodesia. There will be an air display at 11.00 a.m. sharp, which is very impressive. Thank you very much, Ladies and Gentlemen.'

The M.C., who had been waiting for this moment, frantically signalled the band to start playing and they struck up with a fast rumba. But the President had not quite finished his performance. In two strides he crossed to the back of the stage and asked the accordionist, a little man with a toothbrush moustache, if he could borrow his instrument. The request was not denied. Strapping on the Hohner, the Ugandan leader advanced towards the microphone, drawing his instrument in and out, with his long fingers rippling expertly over the keys and a smile of pure childish delight illuminating his face.

## TWO

The glow in the sky thrown up by the floodlighting in the gardens of the great hotel was suddenly extinguished. Michael looked at his watch. It was exactly 2.00 a.m. The signal had been given. In a quarter-of-an-hour it would be time to go. He huddled closer to Ruth for warmth and comfort. They were lying in a sand bunker near the 14th green of the Queen's course, which he had noted on his map of the grounds was known as the 'Witches Bowster.' The name meant little to him, but the words seemed to convey something of the cruel deed he was about to perform. He put the image of the sleeping children from his mind. If he thought about them he would never be able to go through with it. But the length of nylon cord in his packet was an inescapable reminder. He sat up again and shivered. The night had grown cold.

'It is time I was going. Wait for me here until 4.00. I will be back before then, but if I am not . . .'

Ruth reached up a hand and placed it over his mouth. 'I do not want to hear you say anything more.'

'But it is important.' He took hold of her hand and kissed the slim brown fingers. 'You mustn't stay after then. Go back to the car and drive.'

'Oh Michael, don't go, please. Let's leave here now together. This place feels bad. If something happens to you . . . I couldn't live without you.'

She pulled him gently down into the sand and kissed him. 'I want you to forget about it. Let's go away. Please.' She kissed him again hungrily.

'It is no good.' Michael sat up. 'I have to do this . . . I can't give it up now. Ever since I came back from Uganda it has been the most important thing – my whole life. Don't you understand?'

'And what about me? What about us?' Ruth uncurled and rose to her feet, standing over him. 'Isn't that important too?'

Michael said nothing. Without waiting for his answer, Ruth began to undress. Loosening her belt she unzipped the fly of her jeans and pulled them down below her knees. Then she sat down again in the sand and quickly, angrily kicked them off. Reaching out in the dark for his hand she brought it back to her body and pressed it down between her long warm legs. Michael's resistance, already weak, evaporated and with a cry of desperation he buried his head in her lap.

Afterwards Michael said goodbye as casually as if he was going out to the shop to buy a paper. Ruth wept, but for him there could be no other way. He ran up to the lip of the bunker and looked back at her still lying in the sand, a darker shadow against the dune. Then he set off at a fast pace across the golf course towards the hotel.

He followed the route that Sally Temple Owen had outlined for him on the map. The security forces would not try to stop him provided he kept strictly to the approach that had been agreed on. Only a small number of police officers had been briefed about his mission. The fewer, from the Special Branch's point of view, who knew what was going on the better. Finding his way in the dark proved more difficult than it had looked on paper, but after getting lost once over a piece of rough ground that separated the golf courses from the hotel gardens, Michael reached the south wing without incident. As he crossed the grass border and came in close under the walls, the massive structure of Gleneagles loomed threateningly above him.

Moving towards the hotel, he counted four bay windows before he came to the garden door. On either side of it stood two large pots of geraniums. He felt inside the rim of the nearest one and his hand touched cold metal. There were two keys attached to a plastic strip. The larger one fitted the door. He turned it softly in the lock, eased down the handle and let himself into the building.

Inside the door he stood and listened. Apart from the

rumbling of water pipes and the low pitched hum of a generator somewhere in the bowels of the hotel, there was silence. He advanced carefully across the stone flags of the dark hallway and opened a second door into a long dimly lit corridor. Checking first for any sign of movement, he turned left and, passing between a number of shops and a door marked 'Drying Room,' came to the bedroom wing. The carpet was thick-piled and made no sound as he moved quickly along the passage, counting down the even numbers of the rooms.

Outside 234, he stopped and waited again, standing close in to the door to listen for any waking sound, but also in case someone should come by and find him there. He took the keys from his pocket, inserted the Yale in the lock and turned it. Then, with a feeling of dread squeezing at his heart, he opened the door and stepped into the room.

Until this moment he'd thought as little as possible about how he would do the killing. On the way to the Airport Sally had given him a surgical pad and two capsules of chloroform – to make things safer, as well as easier for him. He knew that if one child woke while he was dealing with the other, he was done for. Standing there in the dark vestibule, his hands trembled and with tears in his eyes, Michael crossed himself and prayed for forgiveness for what he was about to do. Then he moved slowly forward into the room.

He took his direction from the sound of the children's breathing and advanced a step at a time until his shins made contact with the bottom of the bed. Holding the surgical pad in one hand, he took the capsules of chloroform from his pocket and broke them over it, then he reached out towards the pillows. He discovered that the children were sleeping together and was glad. It helped too not to know their names. The acrid smell of the chloroform tickled his nostrils. Taking a deep breath he felt for the nearest of the heads on the pillow and held the pad over the child's mouth. He felt the warm soft skin against his hand. The other one began to stir and he quickly transferred the pad. When he had finished the sound of their breathing was deep and regular.

He sat on the edge of the bed, trying to decide whether to

use the cord or a pillow. It was one way of putting off what had to be done. He looked for justification, thinking of Tobias, of Makerere, the death camp in the forest, the hundreds of thousands of his fellow countrymen who had died because of one evil man . . . Time passed. He looked at his watch. It was 2.45. He gave himself another five minutes.

He heard the sound of movement in the next room. The nanny's room. He had forgotten to lock the communicating door. He got up from the bed and moved towards it, but he was already too late. The lights came on, Michael froze as the door to the nanny's room flew open. In its frame, one hand on the light switch, stood a tall grinning figure with thick pink spectacles and tribal scars on his cheeks. Pair of Glasses was holding a gun in his right hand. He fired it. The gun jerked and spat; there was a little flame, but scarcely any sound. Michael felt the impact of the bullet as it struck his shoulder like a massive fist, knocking him back against the bed. General Kitembe's children slept on.

He picked himself up and stumbled towards the window. There was no pain yet. He reached through the curtains with his good arm and felt the cool breath of the night on his face. He thought of Ruth. He got a hand underneath the sash and pushed up. He had to get back to her; she would worry. Another bullet punched into him. It entered half way up his back and smashed through the spinal column.

Michael gave a faint cry, but now his head was already across the sill – he was almost there. He could smell the flowers in the beds below the window. His Ruth was a good girl, she would wait for him. He tried to push himself through, but he couldn't make his body do the right things. His gold-rimmed spectacles fell from his nose. Sorry. The lecture has been delayed . . . She was standing by the banks of the Nile, pale blue and brown . . . he felt himself being pulled back. His chin scraping across the stone. Then his neck was over the sill again and the window coming down, coming down, not all at once but gradually like a slow motion guillotine. As the pressure increased on his throat he began to choke. He saw her again, briefly, then his life was gone.

At the top of the bunker Ruth sat and waited for Michael to come back. She stared through the grey dawn across the misty fairway to the trees, expecting him to appear there at any moment. It was five o'clock. He had told her to go at four. She waited another hour. Still there was no sign of him. At length Ruth got up and, dusting the sand from her jeans, walked back towards the car. She had come to terms with what she had to do.

## THREE

The line of white Cessna 150s, parked on the tarmac in front of the hangars and administration buildings, gleamed in the sunlight. They had been cleaned and fueled and inspected by the mechanics earlier that morning and stood ready for the display. It was perfect weather for flying, the cloud cover high and the wind straight down the runway. Seats for the party of V.I.P.s from Gleneagles had been set out on the grass in front of the Control Tower.

A hundred yards or so from the main airport complex, in its own neatly-kept garden, stood a low white-washed bungalow with the words 'Airschool Services' painted on the roof in large letters. At 10.30 the front door opened and a group of eight black girls in scarlet flying overalls with the Ugandan crest over the breast pocket, each carrying a headset and clipboard, emerged from the building and set off down the gravel path towards the hangars. They seemed nervous and talked among themselves in low whispers. As they reached the gate at the bottom of the garden one of them threw up her hands.

'I've forgotten my met. briefing. Don't wait for me. I'll catch up.' She turned and ran back to the house. The others paid no attention and walked on down to the airfield.

Hidden behind a thicket of gorse at the side of the building, Ruth waited for the girl to reappear. As soon as she heard the footsteps on the porch she called to her softly in her own language. The girl stopped. By now her companions had reached the hangars. She looked about her and then stepped cautiously round to the side of the bungalow.

Ruth called again – this time it was a cry for help. As the girl came nearer, the gorse bush shook and suddenly an arm flew out and grabbed her by the neck. She had no time to cry out. Ruth hit her once with the car jack and the girl fell senseless at her feet. Quickly she pulled her into the bush, stuffed an oil cloth in her mouth and began stripping off her flying suit.

A few minutes later with clipboard under her arm and a headset around her neck Ruth walked out on to the tarmac. Keeping her head low, she ran across to the plane on the end of the line – the only one without a scarlet figure standing beside it – and joined the flight.

The other pilots had already started their pre-flight external checks and were walking around their aircraft looking at the undercarriage, examining the tyres for 'creep,' inspecting wing surfaces, leading edges and flap hinges, testing out the electrics and making sure the engine cowlings, fuel caps, propeller and other moving and removable parts were all secure. Ruth followed their example, opening the pilot's door and checking first that the ignition switches were off. The keys were on the seat. She laid her clipboard with the girl's notes from the met. briefing and instructions for the flypast beside them. An inspection would be held after the flight . . . Memorising the aircraft's registration, B–ABKF (Bravo-Alpha Bravo Kilo Fox), she turned on the Master switch and Pilot Heat tube. Having learnt to fly in a Cessna, she knew her way around the plane; but she hadn't been up since Julian's death and had to concentrate hard. By the time she had completed her checks she had just about caught up with the others. On a signal from the flight leader they climbed aboard their aircraft and closed the doors. A moment later, after a last look at the wireless and V.O.R. aerials, Ruth followed. As she stepped up into the cockpit of Kilo Fox, she noticed through the perspex windscreen, coming along the approach road to the airfield, three long black limousines.

Adjusting the seat so that she could see over the instrument panel and reach full rudder comfortably with her feet, she strapped herself in and from the check list on the clipboard carried out the internal cockpit checks. As soon as she was ready for starting, first looking along the lines of planes to make sure that she was in step with the others, Ruth primed the engine, set the throttle to half-an-inch open and, inserting the key in the magneto switches, turned it to 'both.' The electric starter motor whined and began to turn the propeller, the gauges on the instrument panel flickered and with a muffled bump the Continental engine fired into life. Moving the throttle up a little she set it to 1,000 r.p.m. fast idle for warming. Then she turned on the arionics, electric radio and navigational aid and returned to her check list.

On the grass verge in front of the Control Tower the party of V.I.P.s was moving down from the limousines towards their seats. There was no sign of the children – perhaps Michael had succeeded after all. Her hopes were momentarily raised. But the President was not there either. Ruth's heart missed a beat, then a moment later she saw him coming round the side of the terminal building, wearing a light blue air force uniform and talking expansively to one of the instructors. With a sigh of relief she reached forward and tuned Box One to the Tower frequency. She put on her headphones and adjusting the 'squelch' on the radio, waited for the formation leader to talk to the Tower and reveal the formation call-sign and flight procedure.

'Perth Tower,' the girl's thick Ugandan accents came through loud if not clear, "Dadda leader on one one niner decimal eight, ground check on Box Two.'

'Dadda Leader, Perth Tower receiving you fives,' the controller's voice was smooth and unhurried, 'Roger, to Box One.'

'Perth Tower, Dadda leader, taxi clearance on Box One.'

'Dadda leader, receiving you fives. You are cleared to taxi for Runway 10 left: Fox Echo one zero one three milibars: November Hotel one zero two six milibars.'

'Roger 10 Left, 1013, 1026,' the girl pilot came back.

Ruth noted the numbers down and set her altimeter accordingly. She listened to each member of the formation call the tower to test their radios and confirm the figures, until it was her turn.

'Perth Tower, Dadda 8 on Box One, Runway 10 Left Hand QFE 1013, QNH 1026.' She waited anxiously in case someone noticed her voice was unfamiliar.

'Roger Dadda 8 . . . break, break . . . Dadda Formation is clear to taxi at your discretion.'

She was through. A faint smile crossed her lips as she confirmed the setting. The oil temperature had crept into the green and the pressure needle was beginning to settle. The engine was warming up. She adjusted the cabin heat – it seemed a pointless exercise, but the habits of training were not easily broken.

One by one the Cessnas followed each other down the taxiways to the threshold of Runway 10. Ruth released the brakes, opened the throttle, taxied forward a few feet and checked the toe brake. Then, turning the plane to the right, playing the throttle with one hand on the control yoke, she followed Dadda 7's tail at the 'fast walking pace' that Julian had always gone on about on to the runway. The plane bounced and rocked as it rode over the taxi lights and the perspex windscreen squeaked in its frame. She headed into the wind and put on the brakes for power checks. Open the throttle, take it up smoothly to 1700 r.p.m. . . . Kilo Fox bucked like a stallion as the whirling slipstream of the prop knocked into its own tail and the powerful thrust of the engine tugged against the brakes. Ruth felt the old excitement stirring inside her.

She closed the throttle and began the final pre-take off checks, the 'Vital Actions,' going through them automatically, while she gave careful consideration to the flight. Line astern formation, climbing straight ahead after take off to 500 feet, then turning left away from the buildings, ready for the long left-handed fly-past. It was on that turn that she would have to make her . . . Suddenly she thought of Michael and the tears began to run down her cheeks. She looked over the airfield in case, by some chance . . . but it was no good pretending. She knew what had happened.

The static crackled in her ears. The formation leader was asking for take-off clearance.

'Roger Dadda,' the controller answered, 'you are cleared to line up and hold for a stream take off.'

Slowly, like a string of ducklings making for water, the Cessnas waddled forward on to the tarmac, lining up slightly to the right of each other across the runway to avoid buffeting from the slipstream of the plane in front.

'Dadda is ready for take off.'

'Dadda is cleared for a stream take off. Wind is zero nine zero, seven knots.'

As the flight began to move forward Ruth looked back to the Tower. President Amin was still standing away from the chairs under the shelter of the terminal building. She frowned, wanting him out in the open. The gap between her and the plane in front began to widen. She gave Kilo Fox full throttle and, anticipating the slight swing caused by the sudden surge of power, held the plane straight down the runway. As she gathered speed the frequency at which the wheels drummed over each joint in the concrete increased. Taking her hand off the throttle, she gave the wheel her full attention now as the air moving over the wing surfaces helped them find their independence.

At fifty knots she began to ease back on the stick. The Cessna's nose-wheel became light and the rudder took full directional control. She let the speed build up and gradually felt the plane lift off the ground. The tarmac fell away beneath her. Holding direction, she adjusted altitude and trim and throttled back slightly as the plane attained a positive rate of climb. Passing 150 feet, Ruth selected 'flaps-up' and edged into line behind the wavering conga-like string of aircraft. She could feel the buffets of turbulence caused by the wing vortices and propeller slipstreams in front of her. The Ugandan pilots were not putting on a very impressive performance. But the Cessna was a stable, forgiving animal, designed to fly itself, and now they were all safely up . . . what did it matter? Ruth prayed for strength.

The formation had reached 500 feet and the leader was already turning left to begin the long sweep for the fly-past, when she made her move. At exactly the right moment she shut off the throttle, let the nose drop and banked sharply to the right. The engine cut out and a disconcerting silence filled the cabin. From the ground it would look as if she had an engine failure and was trying to make it back to the air-field – at least that was what she wanted them to think.

She selected hot air on the instrument panel. There was a danger, now that the throttle was closed, of the carbu-rettor icing: at this stage a genuine engine failure would be disastrous. Looking down at the ground she adjusted her rate of turn to get the right position in the sky for a straight run in from behind the hangars. She could see the little group of people in front of the tower and among them now, quite unmistakably, the figure of the President in his light blue uniform, the sun glinting on his medals. With one hand raised to his eyes he watched the flight and searched the sky for the missing aircraft that approached silently from behind him, holding the sun.

The altimeter was unwinding fast. Ruth pushed the nose down and the plane began to gather speed. She eased the throttle on, not wanting to produce engine noise until she was at low level and out of sight behind the hangars. Gravity brought her speed to 130 knots and she felt a sudden surge of exhilaration as she balanced the plane through the steep diving turn. Suspended, almost weightless, pointing straight down at the ground, she descended through 150 feet. Beginning to flatten out the dive, she straightened up on to the final line of approach. At the critical moment she slammed the clod air in and fire-walled the throttle. The plane was approaching the Never Exceed velocity and the engine screamed in protest as the r.p.m. needle shot past the red line on the clock.

She lined up on her target, aiming the aircraft at the row of chairs and the group of people, who were standing now and looking towards her, some beginning to turn away. Ruth pushed hard on the stick to hold the Cessna down as the lift generated by high speed tried to pitch the nose up. The last moments as she held the juddering plane on its destructive course seemed eternal. Buildings, tarmac, grass flashed by in a long mesmerising sweep. In the final second, with the great cowering bulk of the President fixed before her eyes, Ruth cried out. It was a cry of revenge, hatred and exultation, of supreme sacrifice and common deliverance.

Her finger was clamped over the transmit button – the noise from Kilo Fox's cockpit had long since jammed the frequency – and Ruth's cry echoed around the control tower, providing an overture for the explosion, which came a moment later as the plane scythed through the spectators and the fuel tanks burst open and sprayed the area with a shower of fire.

# A PRISONER'S TALE
## by G. F. Newman

Jack Lynn had been well and truly fitted by the filth. And he'd been sentenced to twenty years as a consequence. But Lynn wasn't going to lie still for it. He was going to fight the system every inch of the way, and in every way he knew. Which, in a brutal prison system where lip service is paid to "rehabilitation" but the real name of the game is repression, was a very dangerous strategy. Not that Lynn had much to lose. Or so he thought . . .

*A Prisoner's Tale* uncompromisingly plunges the reader into the world of the modern prison system for one of the most shocking and eye-opening reading experiences of his life. Here, in the form of a savagely compelling novel of desperate men in a desperate situation, is more essential truth about the violent reality of prison existence than could ever be found in a hundred official reports. This outstanding novel concludes G. F. NEWMAN'S frighteningly authentic "Law and Order" trilogy with truly stunning force.

## THE DAY OF RECKONING
by Joe Poyer

Someone was determined to sabotage the most important peace negotiations that America and Russia had ever held. And they were ready to kill mercilessly to achieve their aim. The brutal murder of two young American women . . . a vicious power struggle between two of Russia's most ruthless secret agencies . . . clandestine operations by the CIA right on the Russian border . . . these were just some of the strands in the lethal web of mystery surrounding the plot.
On opposite sides of the world, an FBI agent and a CIA operative raced against time to crack the conspiracy hiding behind the code-name "Day of Reckoning" – before it tore the security of the world apart . . .

THE DAY OF RECKONING is another superb high-tension thriller packed with action and suspense by internationally bestselling author Joe Poyer.

"Plenty of guts . . . a thumping good read"
*Yorkshire Post*

"Mr Poyer is very, very good" *Alistair Mclean*

*Also by Joe Poyer in Sphere Books:*
NORTH CAPE
THE BALKAN ASSIGNMENT
THE CHINESE AGENDA
OPERATION MALACCA

Coming soon!
The shattering thriller of top-level intrigue, corruption and assassination

THE TURNCOAT
by Jack Lynn

1950: Private Gerald Howard Hawthorne, platoon misfit, is decorated for gallantry in action on a Korean battlefield.

1953: Corporal Gerald Howard Hawthorne, prisoner of war, declines repatriation to the USA at the end of hostilities. Branded "the Turncoat" by hysterical witch-hunting media, he "defects" to Red China.

1961: The Turncoat decides to return to the States. And so becomes a human fuse burning inexorably along a terrifying trail of conspiracy and violence towards a political explosion that will rock the White House itself to its deepest foundations . . .

THE TURNCOAT is one of the most frighteningly plausible and compulsively readable political thrillers of the past decade. It is based firmly on events that are known to have taken place but which powerful interests are anxious not to publicise – events of which the author has first-hand knowledge . . . "A fascinating story of Washington cover-up, scandal, intrigue and violence . . . it actually outdoes Forsyth (in these post-Watergate days)" *Tribune*